I0570824

The

Birthday

Gift

The Birthday Gift

a light romance set in Mystic, CT

Virginia Young

Riverhaven Books
www.RiverhavenBooks.com

The Birthday Gift is a work of fiction. While the settings of Mystic, Connecticut, and the surrounding towns are actual, any similarity regarding names, characters, or incidents is entirely coincidental.

Copyright© 2011 by Virginia Young
Original ISBN 978-1-4507-6001-0

All rights reserved.

Published in the United States by Riverhaven Books, Massachusetts.

Reprinted 2012
ISBN 978-1-937588-11-3

Printed in the United States of America

Designed by Stephanie Lynn Blackman
Whitman, MA

In Memory Of
Toby, Pug, and Wolf

Special thanks to
Sesa, Ed, Susan, and Carol
for their editing skills
and
encouragement

Also written by
Virginia Young

Out of the Blue
Sleepless Tides
Winter Waltz
A Family of Strangers

Chapter One

On June 4th, 1973, Cole McGinnis turned five years old. That same day the family next door brought home from the hospital their infant daughter, Jerica Lynn Gates. Dark haired Cole looked at the baby wrapped loosely in a soft, pink blanket and decided that this little girl was his favorite birthday gift. Two years later, the Gates family moved from rural Mystic, Connecticut to the state of Ohio. It was twenty-two years before Cole would see Jerica again.

* * *

"What kind of cake do you want for your birthday?" Mary McGinnis asked her lanky, handsome son as he exchanged her glass storm door for a full-length screen.

"I'll have to think about that one," he said. "It's a toss up. German Chocolate? Carrot cake?"

Mary smiled, one hand on an ample hip. "Well, you think about it and let me know. I have to get the right ingredients you know."

"What about dinner? Don't I get my favorite meal too?"

Mary laughed. "You're too much! You're nearly twenty-nine years old, but sometimes I see you as being about two. So, meatloaf and lots of mashed potato?"

Cole smiled at his mother. "And creamed corn, don't forget the corn." He stood up from making the last adjustment to the door, tried it for smoothness in opening and closing, then stood back and said, "I'm good."

Mary shook her head. "Yes, you are. So, I'll see you here for dinner on Tuesday then?"

"Uh huh. And there'll be presents everywhere, right?"

"You know very well there will be," she said as he hugged her. "All the usual, new slippers and three boxes of your favorite homemade goodies. Someday you're going to think of something new for me to get for you, something exciting."

Cole winked at his mother. "Got a beautiful woman tucked in your closet for me?" And with that he left for his own home, a ten room fixer-upper within walking distance of the sea. He shared his existence with a Golden Retriever and three cats who'd adopted him shortly after he'd bought the house four years earlier. He loved the antique woodwork, the crown moldings, the wide plank floors, and the old and luscious plantings outside. It was a constant effort, but still, his dream home.

Cole showed up at his mother's house on Tuesday. It would be just the two of them; his father had been gone for several years, the car crash victim of a drunk driver.

"Everything smells fantastic, Mom," Cole said entering the kitchen. He stopped short at the sight of a very pretty young woman at the sink next to his mother.

"Cole, you remember this lovely girl? This is little Jerica, the baby you fell in love with twenty-four years ago."

Cole stepped back, amazed at the memory and at the beautiful girl before him. Her eyes were the brightest blue he'd ever seen, and her honey hair was long, past her shoulders. She was a definite knockout.

"Hi," she said as she smiled and extended her hand.

Cole moved forward and took her hand briefly, then stepped back. "You've grown considerably," he said.

"Honey," his mother began with a chuckle, "babies don't stay little, you know. Jerica is twenty-four now. She's through with college and works in administration for St. Joe's Hospital."

"Here in Mystic?" he asked.

"Yes," Mary McGinnis answered excitedly, not giving the young woman a chance to speak, "right here in Mystic."

Cole looked at Jerica and she smiled. "I've been here for about a month, just settling in actually."

2

Cole shifted from his left foot to his right. "Didn't your family move out of state?"

"Ohio, yes. They're still there, but they might be moving back East. Dad's getting ready to retire and they've always wanted to come back to Connecticut. I'm making it easier for them by taking this job at St. Joseph's."

Cole nodded; he still couldn't believe his eyes.

"I should get going," Jerica said. "I just wanted to stop in and say hello from the Gates family. Mom and Dad have fond memories of living here, and of both of you, of course. They were very saddened to learn of your loss. They said that Mr. McGinnis was a wonderful man."

"You're welcome to stay for dinner," Mary McGinnis said. "It's Cole's birthday today."

Cole felt slightly embarrassed with that announcement but smiled as Jerica wished him a very happy birthday. Within moments, she was gone, leaving behind her soft scent and a distinct look of interest on Cole's face. Some birthday present.

Mary watched her son's eyes follow Jerica to her car. "She's grown to be a beautiful girl," she commented.

Cole turned and asked, "So, dinner ready?"

Two weeks later, Cole stopped at his mother's house to drop off a basket of fresh peaches and to invite her to a movie. He had his own life, but he was aware that his mother had to be lonely at times living on her own. At fifty-seven, she was still beautiful and filled with an incredible energy for life. Her job as a second-grade teacher in the town's elementary school made her someone just about everyone knew.

He set the peaches on the counter next to the sink then hollered out to her.

"We're upstairs, Honey. Come on up."

Cole hesitated. Who was upstairs with his mother? He climbed the stairs two at a time and found himself face to face with his mother and Jerica Gates.

"Well, hi," he said. "Sorry to have interrupted you two. I didn't see another car in the driveway."

"My car is in for repairs," Jerica said. "Your mother was kind enough to offer me a lift when she saw me walking."

"I've also asked Jerica to stay for dinner. Will you join us?" she asked her son.

Cole looked from one to the other. He'd intended to watch a baseball game with a cold beer and a pizza, but this invitation could prove to be more interesting. "Yeah, sounds good," he said.

In the kitchen, Mary put Jerica to work making a salad while Cole cut peaches to be topped with vanilla ice cream. Mary mixed a batch of buttermilk biscuits and a pitcher of iced mint tea. The meal was light and delicious, served out on the patio with a view of Mary's graceful weeping willow and a pair of brown rabbits who found tiny carrots waiting for them beneath the long, protective branches.

After they'd eaten, chatting amiably, Jerica offered to do the dishes before she walked home. "Cole can help me," she said with a smile.

Mary laughed at the look on her son's face. He wasn't used to meandering about in the kitchen; cutting peaches had been his planned contribution of help.

"You laugh," he said to his mother, "but I can handle this. Who do you think washes up at my house?"

"Since when do you wash paper plates?" Mary asked, still laughing.

Cole gave her a stern glance then stood up and collected the dishes while Jerica stood and carried a tray of glasses toward the kitchen. "You stay and relax, Mary," she said to the older woman. "Keep an eye on those little bunnies out there."

In the kitchen, Cole and Jerica collided at one point and, while she laughed, he felt incredibly clumsy.

"Sorry," he said, "but don't tell my mother. She already thinks I'm inept at this kitchen stuff."

Laughing, Jerica handed Cole a dishtowel to dry the dishes she washed.

"How is it being back here?" he asked.

"It's good. I liked being in college here in Connecticut, seeing my grandparents in their final years, and a few other relatives, but being back in Mystic again, near the sea, back to the very place where I was born, is great. What about you? Did you ever leave?"

4

"Yeah, I went to college in Boston. I came home summers, always knew I wanted to live here. Besides, my mother's alone, so I wouldn't have considered living anywhere else."

"She told me you're an avid sailor, that you teach sailing to kids."

"That's right," Cole said as he dried dishes and placed them onto the shelves where they belonged. "I teach history at the high school and sailing is a course I offer during the summer months while school is out."

"That sounds like a great way to spend the summer. Maybe someday I'll learn to sail; it looks so romantic."

"It might, but it's also a lot of hard work," he said.

"Okay," Jerica said as she looked at the sparkling kitchen, "we've done it. Now, I really need to get going. I have a report to work on for tomorrow."

"How far are you from here? Need a ride?"

"That would be great. My apartment is probably not more than a mile away, but a ride sounds very inviting."

Together they walked out onto the patio and said thank you and good night to Mary as she sipped the last of her tea.

Cole and Jerica climbed into his Jeep and drove out of the driveway.

"Your mother issued an invitation to me," Jerica began after a few minutes. "I was telling her that my apartment is small and expensive. She asked if I'd like to move into her house with her. Do you have any feelings about that? She's wonderful, but I don't want to put her out in any way." Jerica pointed to a small apartment building and Cole stopped before its front entrance.

"I guess I'm kind of surprised. I never thought of Mom renting out a room or anything like that, but I can't say it's a bad idea. I worry about her being alone. Are you giving this concept some consideration?"

"I don't know. She mentioned it when we got to the house and then she took me upstairs to show me the three bedrooms. She said that she sleeps in the downstairs bedroom, so I could use the three rooms and the bath upstairs. It doesn't sound like we'd be in one another's way, so maybe, unless you can think of why I shouldn't."

Cole shifted the Jeep into park and looked at Jerica's beautiful face. "I can't think of a reason in the world," he said. "Do you have a lot of stuff to move if you decide to? I'd be glad to give you a hand."

Jerica smiled. "Thanks, but I have very little. The apartment came furnished, so it's just my personal effects and me. I'm really going to think about it though. Your mother is so nice, and living there, with that heavenly yard, would certainly be more enjoyable than living on the third floor of an apartment building. Thanks for the ride, Cole. Maybe I'll see you soon."

"Probably," he said, "and you're welcome. It was my pleasure."

He watched her walk away into the arched entryway of the building, her long pink skirt and white blouse slightly transparent and very appealing. He pulled away with a smile on his face. Jerica moving into his mother's house was a very nice idea, he thought. It would be good for his mother, good for Jerica, and not such a bad idea for him either. He drove toward his country-style home, recalling the baby he'd fallen in love with so many years ago. After she'd moved, he'd begged his parents to get her back, and although Jerica wasn't a constant on his mind over the years, he'd never forgotten her. Now here she was, back in his life.

Three weeks later, Jerica had managed to find someone to sublet her apartment. Freeing her from the rent she'd promised to pay for one year, she moved into the home of Mary McGinnis. Cole stopped in briefly that evening on his way to a baseball game and found his mother and Jerica sharing a meal of grilled cheese and tomato sandwiches and his mother's prize-winning coleslaw with bits of apple grated in with the cabbage. He wouldn't have minded staying and having some of that, but he was meeting friends and needed to go. Seeing the two of them together, he felt comforted; Jerica's coming back was a great stroke of luck.

"I feel so fortunate to have this opportunity to be with you, Mary," Jerica said as they enjoyed their iced tea after supper. "I really didn't like it at the apartment; it wasn't homey at all. Thank you again for having me here."

"You don't need to say another word, Jerica. I love the company; I think this is going to work out just fine. By the way," she began,

6

"what's a sweet young thing like you doing unattached? Isn't there someone in the picture?"

Jerica nodded. "Yes, there is. His name is Dan Walters. We've known one another since college. I'm sure you'll meet him sometime. He lives in Hartford and works in the insurance industry there."

Mary nodded. "Is this serious? Are you two talking marriage?"

Jerica smiled. "He's popped the question once or twice. I'm giving it some thought. We'll see."

Mary didn't ask any more questions; she'd leave it to Jerica to bring up the subject again.

"Would you mind if I went upstairs for the evening, Mary? I thought I'd shower before I work on my reports for awhile."

"You go right ahead. I'll see you in the morning. If you're up before me, help yourself to whatever you can find. There's fruit and there's a couple of kinds of cereal, or bread for toast. You have whatever you'd like."

"This is fantastic," the young woman said. "It's just like home." She gently touched Mary on the shoulder and left the patio to go upstairs.

A few days later, on Saturday morning, Cole arrived with the back of his Jeep filled with bags of mulch. One by one he unloaded them onto the driveway, then opened them and began to spread the rich, dark substance around the shrubs and flower gardens. Jerica saw him working from her upstairs window and decided to go down and say hi. Wearing pale green shorts and a cream colored jersey, she was careful when walking in her bare feet.

"Good morning," she greeted him. "You're out and about early."

"Yeah, well, I meant to get more mulch on these gardens earlier in the spring. I tried to get more but they'd run out of it, so when I saw this new load come in to the nursery, I grabbed some. I need more at my place too. How are things going here? You all settled in?"

"Yes, it's great. Your mother is so easy to get along with. I love it here. Where's your place? Your mother said you have a country house."

Cole laughed. "Yeah, it's an ongoing creation. I love the place. It's old and historic, but two of the rooms - the kitchen and family room - are fairly new. I had a new electric service put in, new plumbing, and a new roof. The furnace was new when I bought the house. The rest of the work is cosmetic, and I'm taking care of that myself."

"I'd like to see it sometime," she said.

Cole wiped his brow with the back of his hand. "I can arrange that. What are you doing tomorrow? Maybe you and Mom could come out for lunch."

"That sounds wonderful. I'd love it."

Cole watched as Jerica walked toward the side door of his mother's house, stopping to pick a dandelion on the way. She was a nice little package: pretty, intelligent, sweet, and just the right amount of sassy. He seemed to find it slightly frightening to think of being this interested, understanding that she could go away again. What if her parents didn't make the move from Ohio? What if she decided to return there to be with them? Then what? Cole went back to mulching the gardens, convinced that he really had to put this girl out of his thoughts. Not completely out, that would be impossible; after all, she lived at his mother's. But thinking of her in a romantic way could prove to be a heartbreaker.

When the mulch had been spread, Cole walked into the bathroom and decided to take a quick shower to get the dust and dirt off before his mother came home, and then he'd extend the invitation for lunch at his place for tomorrow. No harm in lunch, especially with his mother around. He closed the bathroom door and ran the water until the temperature was right, then he stripped out of his clothes and stepped into the warm spray. When the combination of perspiration and dirt were washed away, Cole turned the water off and reached outside for a towel. He was annoyed with himself for not checking to see that a large bath towel was handy before he stepped into the shower. There was none. Just a washcloth and a dainty little hand towel. Cole brushed the water from his eyes and stepped out just as Jerica walked into the bathroom. Stunned, he could see from the shock on her face that she had no idea he stayed after finishing with the mulching. Accustomed to taking a shower at his mother's house when he did gardening and other chores for her, he hadn't stopped to think about her new housemate and he was both embarrassed and surprised by his new situation.

Her eyes fixed on him, Jerica stammered, "Excuse me, I'm so sorry," and hastily retreated to the other side of the bathroom door.

Cole stepped back into the shower behind the muted glass doors. She had, he decided, probably seen nothing but the left side of his body, his leg and his torso. But it was still embarrassing. He found a large towel in the vanity cupboard and wrapped himself in it. Now he had to make his way to one of the upstairs bedrooms, the one that had been his, where he kept a few clean garments. His mother had always said they'd come in handy when he worked around her house. But then, there was Jerica. How was he going to get past her since she occupied the whole upstairs?

He stood in the bathroom smoothing his thick, black hair back with one hand while the other held the towel in place on his hips.

"Cole?"

"Yeah," he answered.

"I am so sorry. I didn't know you were in there."

"Uh huh, I know. Um, could you do me a favor? Unless I come out in this towel, or put my grubby clothes back on, I have nothing to wear. Could you go upstairs to the blue room and bring me a shirt and jeans?"

"Sure."

He could hear her footsteps on the stairs. He shook his head, thinking that this was unbelievable. When she came back and knocked on the door, he opened it just about two inches.

"Found them okay, I see."

"Yes, well that's my room now. I liked the color, so I moved your clothes over to one side of the closet to make room for mine."

Cole pulled the clean garments on quickly then stepped out of the bathroom in bare feet, his sneakers in his hands. "Thanks," he said, "I should have thought about it before I showered - I'm just so used to roaming around here like I did when I was a kid."

Jerica smiled and nodded. "That's understandable. I'm sure I'd do the same at my parents' home."

"Well," Cole began, "I was going to wait around for Mom, to extend the lunch invitation for tomorrow, but maybe I'll hit the road and call her later."

"Okay. And is there something I can bring for lunch? I'd be happy to pick something up at the bakery downtown, or I could make a salad."

Cole looked at her. Man, she is not only gorgeous but as cool as a cucumber, as though she never saw me naked. "Just show up," he said. "Leave the fixings to me. I promise: I can cook."

"Sounds like the perfect man," she said with a bright smile.

On Sunday, Mary and Jerica arrived at Cole's home around one, just in time for the warm sun to settle behind his three large maples. The bright green trees provided a nice area of shade for their Adirondack chairs and spiked lemonade.

"What's in this?" Mary asked after swallowing some of the pale pink beverage. "It has a bite to it."

Cole chuckled. "Just a tad of gin, enough to make you smile."

Mary frowned at her handsome son. "Sure, get your mother drunk, that's nice."

"Mom," he said, "if you get drunk on that whole pitcher of lemonade, you'd still be the cheapest date anyone ever had. There's so little alcohol in that drink, it's practically all your imagination."

Mary winked at Jerica. "Come on, we'll take a tour of the house while Cole cooks. He won't tell you half what he's done here, so I'll point it out to you. I think it's really charming."

"I can see that already," Jerica said. "It's a wonderful old place. I can understand why you love it here, Cole."

"Thanks," he said, and as the two women disappeared from his patio, he pulled a lasagna from the oven, tossed more grated cheese on the top, and left it to settle on the stove. As the salad was chilling in the refrigerator, he set the table and placed rolls and butter in a basket on the red table cloth. His mother had taught him well.

While waiting for them to return, Cole took his lemonade out to the patio and tossed a frisbee to Murphy, his Golden Retriever, then he gave him a fresh bowl of water and a small dog biscuit. The cats were indoor inhabitants, most likely sleeping in one of the upstairs rooms or maybe watching the birdfeeders from the living room window.

"This house is amazing," Jerica said as she entered the kitchen and then onto the patio through a screen door. "I love it. It has everything. I'm very impressed with your carpentry skills."

"Thanks," he said. "Where's Mom? Did she get lost?"

"I'm right here," Mary said as she joined them on the patio. "I stopped to see Maybelle and Gertrude. They were enjoying a nap in the front bedroom. Then I had to find Edgar, of course. He was staking his claim in the red room, stretched out in the window against the screen. Such spoiled little creatures."

Cole smiled. "Yup, just like you taught me. So, are you two hungry? The lasagna is ready and the rolls are on the table. I'll get the salad. There's more lemonade, or there's coffee, tea, whatever you'd like."

Jerica wasn't sure she'd ever felt this content before. She looked from mother to son. What a wonderful pair they are. I wonder how different life would have been if I'd grown up here in Mystic, near the sea, near Cole. "I'm famished," she said, and they all went to the table for a delicious meal and companionable conversation. They ate, shared stories, and, after adjourning to the patio with their coffee, were offered dessert: strawberries with whipped cream. They each had some and then Mary suggested that since they all had to work the next day, they should be going. On the patio, as Mary fetched her purse from the inside, Jerica thanked Cole for a wonderful afternoon and a gourmet meal. "It's really fabulous here, Cole. I wish I could stay forever."

He smiled and then his mother stepped out onto the patio to say thank you and goodnight. Mother and son embraced as Jerica looked on, wishing that the embrace might include her as well. She remembered the moment in Mary's bathroom and felt herself blush. The air was heavy with the memory of that instant, like a perfectly formed marble finding its way to the bottom of a water filled glass, silent, but predominately, predictably there.

Cole stayed his distance over the next few days with only a periodic phone call to his mother. After the fourth day had passed and he hadn't stopped in, she phoned him and invited him to supper. He was hesitant, then she begged. "Come on, I'll be alone tonight. Jerica is out for the evening and I'll make baked chicken with stuffing. Come and have a meal with your mother."

"All right," he said, eased to know that it would be just the two of them.

Mary was a wonderful cook and the dinner was delicious. When they'd finished she asked, "Would you like iced tea and lemon meringue pie out on my porch?"

"I'm stuffed, Mom," he said. "How about if I take a piece of pie home? I'll have the iced tea though."

Mary agreed and poured two frosty glasses of tea as they sat down in white wicker rockers on the porch.

"You haven't even asked where Jerica is tonight," Mary said. "Aren't you curious? She's usually here."

Cole looked at his mother. "Okay, where is she? Working late?"

Mary shook her head from side to side. "No, she's out with her friend."

Cole nodded. "That's good. Have you met this friend?"

"Oh, yes. He came to pick her up."

"He? I didn't know she was seeing anyone."

Cole felt his stomach tighten and tried to make sure his voice didn't reflect the emotion he felt.

Mary looked at her handsome son. His dark hair was so like his father's, but Cole was a combination of Mary's brother and her deceased husband, inheriting the best of their features. She knew he felt more for Jerica than he'd admit and suspected he'd stayed away for that very reason.

"I know you like Jerica, Honey, but guard your heart. She has someone in her life and I don't want to see you get hurt. Seems to me you've already had enough of that with Linda. I think this fellow, Dan, is pretty significant to Jerica."

"Don't worry about me, Mom. I'm okay," he said.

Mary sipped her iced tea and wondered. Cole had everything going for him, but he'd been hurt before and all she wanted for him was the best.

On his drive home that night, Cole felt like everything he'd had for dinner was stuck like a four-inch rock in a two-inch hole. Somewhere in the deep folds of his mind, Jerica Gates had always been there. She'd been taken away as a toddler, now here she was, in full glory, but taken. What was he going to do with what he felt for her? What did he have a right to do? Nothing. Cole felt a sense of sadness that she could slip away again. Why would it be in any way fair for her to have walked back into his life, only to walk right back out? None of it made sense. He didn't want it to make sense. He wanted Jerica, and he thought he just might fight for her.

Chapter Two

"Hey, Jerica," he said in an early morning telephone call. "Good morning. Interested in coffee at Pete's Café? He makes the best bagels anywhere, and if you prefer something sweet, he also makes the best Danish pastry. Say yes."

Jerica laughed. "I have a ton of work to do. I should have done it last night, but I didn't, plain and simple."

Yeah, and I know why you didn't, you were out with Dan. .Aloud he said, "Come on. It's coffee, not a seven-course meal. It won't take that long."

She laughed again. "What's this all about anyway?"

Cole hesitated and closed his eyes for a moment. "Just like the idea of starting my day off right, that's all."

Jerica was silent, a little stunned at his announcement.

"Does that dead air space mean no?" he asked.

Jerica smiled into the phone. "No," she said. "I'll meet you at Pete's in twenty minutes. But I'm serious; I need to get these reports done. I won't have a lot of time."

"See you in twenty," he said, then placed the phone back on its receiver. He looked down at his bare chest and decided he'd better get a shirt on. He chose a pale blue, one of his favorites. He ran his fingers through his dark hair, grabbed his car keys and left the house.

On the drive to Pete's Café, Cole was both excited about the prospect of seeing Jerica and apprehensive about the future. Aside from Linda, who had found an attraction to a prominent young attorney, there had been very few love interests for him. If this Dan was a serious contender, Cole wasn't sure if there was anything he could do, or even if there was anything he wanted to do. Why would he mess with Jerica's feelings?

He pulled his Jeep into the small restaurant's parking lot and she was there, wearing a navy blue skirt and a pale blue blouse, her blonde hair moving gently in the morning breeze.

"Hi," she said as she walked toward him.

"Good morning," he said. "Thanks for meeting me."

They walked into the café together and found a booth. The waitress approached them with a glass coffee pot in her hands and two mugs. "Coffee?" she asked.

"Yes, please," they said in unison.

The waitress nodded and left two menus on the table with the promise of getting right back to them to take their order.

"So," Jerica began, "is everything okay? I mean, your mother, is she still all right with me living at her house? I'd hate to think I've done something to offend her."

"No, no, nothing like that at all. Mom loves having you there. No, I just thought it would be fun to have breakfast together. I didn't mean to frighten the daylights out of you."

Jerica smiled and pushed her long hair back from her shoulders. "You didn't, I guess I'm over-sensitive about some things. So, this is just a social meeting then? This is nice."

"Yeah, I thought so. So, how's life in general? Is the work at the hospital interesting?"

"You know," Jerica began as she stirred cream and sugar into her coffee, "it's very involved. I do find it interesting, but there are times when I question my motives to get into administrative work. I wish I'd thought more about the mountains of paperwork and the lack of communication with other people. I don't know, maybe I'll figure out a career change for myself, or maybe I'll adjust to what I have. I need to give it a chance. What about you? Is teaching something you always wanted to do?"

"No," Cole said with a smile. "I think it was always in the back of my mind though. It wasn't until I'd finished college and was working with a computer company that I decided to think about something else to do with my life. I thought about being an architect, then a friend suggested exploring teaching and I gave it some serious thought. I went back to school, got certified, and here I am. I like it a lot; I like the kids. Not real sure I'll stay at the high school level, however. I'm working on getting my Master's - I need to finish that, so there's a chance I'll eventually teach at the college level. I've heard that teaching college is more satisfying because the victims don't have to be disciplined, you can actually teach."

Jerica laughed. "I understand completely."

The waitress arrived with her note pad and took their orders for bagels with creamed cheese and a shared dish of sliced melon.

"Can I ask you something personal?" he asked when the waitress had gone.

"Sure. Go ahead," Jerica said. "I might choose not to answer though."

Cole nodded and smiled. "That's fair. I was just wondering what's going on in your personal life. Mom mentioned you were seeing someone. Is this a serious relationship?"

Jerica sipped her warm coffee and made room for the bagels and fruit. "I've known Dan for a few years, we were in college together. He's great, really a nice guy. As far as the question about having a serious relationship, I guess it is. Dan would like us to get married. In his mind, I think he imagines we're already engaged."

"What about you? Are you thinking that way too?"

Jerica swallowed a small piece of bagel then took another sip of coffee. "I'm not sure. I think I should be sure, but then again, I think I'd miss him if he wasn't around. We've been together a long time."

"So, you're dating him exclusively?"

"Oh, yes. I'm a one-guy-at-a-time person. I could never juggle two romances. What about you? Who's special in your life?"

Cole put his coffee mug down and looked at her. "No one right now." But in his heart, he knew he was telling an untruth; Jerica Gates was very, very special.

Having breakfast and easy conversation with her felt so natural that he didn't want those precious minutes to end. When she gathered her purse and car keys and thanked him for a nice way to start the day, he stood and walked with her out to the car.

"I'm glad you could meet me," he said, his hand on her door.

"Me too. Maybe we could do it again sometime. In fact, if you invite us over for breakfast, I'll make you French Pancakes. Ever have them?"

Cole smiled. "Are those little round things with the escargot syrup?"

Jerica shuddered. "No escargot. And, no syrup, just salt and butter, and they're wonderful. Invite your mother and me: I'll make them. You'll love them."

"You've got a deal," he said, and then he closed her car door and she started the engine. He watched her drive away and felt a heaviness settle in his heart. Please don't like Dan so much, he thought as he watched the car disappear around the corner.

That evening, Mary McGinnis called Cole and asked if he could find the time to plant a lilac tree she'd been given that day at work. "Deena had these lilacs and wanted to thin them out. You know how I love them - I couldn't resist."

"Okay," he said, "I'll pop over in an hour or so. You'd better have something to reward me with."

"Will brownies do? I made some last night."

"You know me too well, Mom. I'll be over in a little while." It would be a chance to see Jerica again. Jerica and brownies - not a bad combination. He walked Murphy, fed the cats, then drove to his mother's house. As he pulled into the driveway, he could see that Jerica's car wasn't there and it left him with an empty feeling.

The lilac was planted near to the house where Mary could best enjoy its subtle fragrance, and then the brownies were served with iced tea.

"Where's your star boarder tonight?" he asked casually.

"She went right after work to meet her 'intended'. I don't like that; he should be picking her up. If she goes to meet him, that means she gets to drive herself home later. That's not the way we did it in my day. Men always came to the house."

Cole sat back in his chair. He'd consumed one brownie and was enjoying his cold tea. Thoughts of Jerica had to be squelched. She was seeing someone else.

"What about you, Honey," Mary asked. "What ever happened to that cute little Sara Haskins you dated? You never mention her anymore."

Cole shrugged. "Sara's nice. There weren't exactly fire works with her; I think we both realized that. She was seeing someone the last I heard."

Mary shook her head. "How am I gonna get a grandchild that way? I'm not getting any younger, you know."

Cole smiled. "Yup, me neither, Mom. Listen, I'm taking off now unless you need me for something else. I have my new summer sailing class to plan. Don't forget to water that lilac before you go to work in the morning." He stood, kissed his mother goodbye, and left.

It was starting to get dark and he wondered where Jerica was. When he walked into his house, locking the door behind him, he ruffled Murphy's ears and the dog followed him to the recliner in the living room where Cole sat with his books on sailing. He closed his eyes for a moment. He loved that house, his pets, seeing his mother frequently, but there was definitely something missing. Jerica. Jerica Gates was missing from this otherwise perfect scene.

A few days passed and although Cole had spoken with his mother on the phone, he'd stayed away from her house and the agony of seeing Jerica. When the phone rang after nine at night, he assumed it was his mother and was surprised to find Jerica's voice on the phone.

"Am I calling too late?" she asked.

"No," Cole said as he shifted himself in his recliner, "not at all. Is everything okay?"

"Oh, yes," Jerica said. "Everything is fine. I was calling to ask about the weekend. I have it free and was wondering if you'd like to do that French Pancake breakfast I told you about. Maybe on Sunday? That is, if you have the time. I mentioned it to your mom and she's up for it too."

Cole threw his head back and closed his eyes. He wanted that time with her, but just how free was her weekend? Free for a couple of days? Was that enough for him - stolen hours here and there?

"Sure," he said, "it sounds great. Would you like to prepare your feast here or there?"

18

Jerica laughed. "Well, you know I love it here, but I'm dying to get back over to your place. Would you mind us messing up your kitchen?"

"No problem," he said, his heart beating wildly. "What do I need to have on hand?"

"Nothing, I'm bringing the ingredients with me. It's very simple, basic stuff, but you're going to love it."

Cole smiled. "I'm sure I will." After the call, he invited Murphy for a walk on that wonderfully moonlit night. He didn't try not thinking of her; even in small increments, she was worth his thoughts. I give in, he thought, she's just too fantastic to push away. And then he wondered: had she ever made those French Pancakes for Dan?

Sunday couldn't come fast enough. Cole bought a small Boston Fern he could plunk in the middle of the table and used a set of blue and white dishes that had belonged to his grandparents. It looked nice and fresh. As he stood back from the table, wondering if he'd forgotten anything, the door to the kitchen creaked open and there stood Jerica, a bowl of strawberries in her hands and a smile on her pretty face.

"Hey," Cole said, "how're you doing? Where's Mom?"

Jerica placed the strawberries on the counter next to the sink and left her shoulder purse and car keys on a chair. "Your Mom had a call from her friend, the one who gave her the lilacs. She's hurt her knee and your mother is going there to make her breakfast and visit. She said to tell you that if you lived through the pancakes, she'd try them sometime!"

Cole smiled. "Great. Nice mother. Okay, so come on in and make yourself at home. I've got fresh coffee. Want a cup?"

"Sure. I'll be right back. I left the bag of stuff in the car; just toss one sugar and a bit of cream in my coffee and I'll love you forever." Then she was gone.

If only it were that simple, he thought.

Jerica came back into the kitchen as if it were her own and placed a brown paper bag on the counter top. "Is it all right if I use that blue bowl on top of your frig?" she asked as Cole handed her a cup of coffee.

"Whatever you need," he said and reached for the bowl to place it before her. She sipped the coffee and sighed, then placed the cup down and began to unpack the ingredients she'd brought with her.

"You know," he began with a smile, "I have all of those things in the house."

"Yes, but I'm making you breakfast. I didn't think it was right to use your supplies."

Cole smiled, "May I help?"

"Yes, you can watch. This is a very simple recipe. You're going to want it again and I might not be around to prepare it for you, so take a note or two, and you'll see how to make them. First," she began, "we need flour in the bowl, then we need sugar. Add salt, and mix those three dry ingredients together. When they're nice and smooth, we're going to melt some butter." She stopped and placed butter into a microwavable measuring cup and heated it for about fifteen seconds. She added the butter to the dry mixture, then cracked five eggs into the bowl. She beat them quickly with a fork until the thick blend was smooth, then gradually added a little more than a cup of milk until the batter was thinned. "There, that's it," she said as she mixed the pale yellow substance. "Now, we need a frying pan or griddle. What do you have?"

"Both," Cole said. "The griddle goes across two of the burners."

"Good, I'll take the griddle. We'll use a nice dollop of butter, and when that's melted, we start spooning out the batter into about six-inch diameter pancakes. When they're done, and it only takes a few minutes because they're thin, you eat them drenched in butter and salt. And by the way, I didn't say they weren't loaded with calories, I just said they're good."

"They smell fantastic," he said as he stood near to her and watched the pancakes turning into a golden brown. She took one aside, rolled it in butter, shook a bit of salt on it, and gestured for him to open his mouth.

Cole took a bite then closed his eyes and chewed. After he'd swallowed the last of it he said, "Wow, they're really great. It's amazing how something so simple could taste so good."

Jerica smiled brightly. "I know. I'll cook up a dozen or so, then we can sit down with our coffee and strawberries too." She turned to look at him after she'd flipped six small pancakes. "Thanks for letting me do this, Cole. This is my idea of fun."

"I'm the one who should thank you. These things are terrific, and you're right, I'll want them again."

As she continued to cook, he poured more coffee and thought about how much he was loving this moment, this girl.

After breakfast, they cleaned the kitchen together and then Cole invited Jerica to walk outside with Murphy and him, exploring the gardens and old bushes.

"This yard has so many pretty plants and flowering shrubs," she said. "It reminds me of an older person's home. Everything looks so established."

"The house belonged to an older woman, a widow and former librarian in town. She was nearly ninety when she decided to go and live with a daughter far away. I wish I could claim planting the nice things here, but she did it all. It was part of what called to me when I decided to buy this house."

Jerica stole a glance at him and her heart skipped more than a beat. He was rugged looking, but sweet and handsome. She wondered how he'd escaped the arms of someone all these years, but she wasn't going to ask. That would sound like a leading question and her position was with Dan. Dan, she'd never made French Pancakes for Dan, and now she wondered why.

"Your mother said you were about twenty-five when you found this place. Most guys that age are out doing the club scene, not looking for the responsibility of a house."

Cole smiled. "Yeah, well it was a matter of timing. I'd been thinking I needed to be a little more independent, and at the same time, this house became available." Cole tossed a tennis ball to Murphy who chased after it and caught it in mid air. "Good show, Murph," he said as the dog returned the ball. Cole tossed it again, this time a little further into the yard. "I kept looking at my mother and wondering if she'd ever consider a new relationship. With me around, that was unlikely."

Jerica nodded. "She's great. I'll bet there are lots of men who'd like your mother's company."

"Absolutely. One of my Dad's old friends, Jim, I know he'd love to catch my mother's eye. Problem is I think she sees him as more of a brother figure. We'll see, maybe I'm stepping into her business and shouldn't, but at least I'm out of the way."

They moved closer to the patio where Murphy joined them and stretched out in a shady patch on cool flagstones.

"Can you stay a while?" Cole asked. "I'll get you another cup of coffee."

Jerica agreed. "Great, but this time, would you add a few ice cubes for me? It's warm enough that I think iced coffee would hit the spot."

"Good idea," he said, "I'll have one of those too. Sit down and make yourself comfortable; I'll be right back."

Cole returned with two tall glasses of iced coffee and sat in the chair next to Jerica. When she accepted the frosty glass from him, their fingers touched and lingered moments longer than perhaps they should have.

"So, how come you had the weekend free? Aren't you usually doing something with your friend?" He couldn't bring himself to say the name, Dan.

Jerica swallowed a few sips of the coffee and then replied, "Usually, but this weekend he was going with his brother and a few friends white water rafting."

"Not your thing?" Cole asked with a smile.

"I don't know, I've never been. But this is something they do together for a male bonding or something. I didn't mind him going."

Cole took a long swallow of the coffee and wondered why any man fortunate enough to have Jerica Gates would want to go off with other guys.

"Am I keeping you from getting on with something else?" she asked turning to look him straight in the eyes. "I came to make you breakfast, but I didn't mean to take up your whole day."

"You're not keeping me from anything important. When you have a home, there's always something to do, but it'll wait. This is really pretty nice; I like this."

Jerica's beautiful blue eyes looked into Cole's of deep brown. "Thanks, I like it too. It's so peaceful here. I really like Mystic, and the name, well what could be more intriguing than the name Mystic?"

Cole laughed. "You're right. It's a neat name." Then he glanced at her and thought she looked tired. "That chair you're in goes back with a little push if you're feeling like a snooze."

Jerica rubbed her eyes. "That would be so rude of me. I am tired - I didn't sleep well last night. I've been trying to work on a contract for work and it's complicated. Sometimes I don't know why I chose this career path."

"What would you rather be doing?" he asked.

Jerica sighed. "Almost anything. I like the hospital, but my work is all with paper. It leaves me feeling like just another machine. I used to think of being an interior decorator," she said with a smile, "but Mom and Dad thought that was risky and frivolous. They're right, I know, but it still sounds like a fun way to use your life." She yawned and stretched back in the reclining chair. "If I fall asleep, first of all, I will be most apologetic, but also, please wake me."

"Close your eyes for a few minutes," Cole suggested. "A nap will do you good."

"Okay," she said, and within moments, she was asleep, her head turned to the side. Cole watched her breathe and thought she was quite possibly the most beautiful thing he'd ever seen. After several minutes, he stood and walked to his shed where he stored his garden tools. He could work in the yard while she dozed. More than an hour later, he returned to the patio to find her still soundly asleep. He went into the house and took a sheet from his linen closet, using it to cover her bare arms and legs. He was tempted to press his lips to hers, but there was Dan to consider.

When she awoke, Jerica blinked against the summer sun setting in the west. She looked at her watch and was horrified to realize that she'd been asleep for hours. She sat up and looked around, finding Cole at the edge of his property, clipping some rhododendrons. She stood, folded the sheet and placed it in the chair before walking to him.

"I'm so sorry," she began. "I've never done anything like that before. I must have been exhausted."

Cole stopped clipping and looked at her with a smile. "No problem. I figured you needed the sleep. It was nice to look back and see you there. In fact, Murph stayed by your side for the first couple of hours."

23

"I'm embarrassed," she said. "I should be going. I'm really sorry about this."

"Don't be," he said, "there's nothing to be sorry for. Anyway, what's your hurry? We skipped lunch, I actually had another coffee, but now I'm ready for dinner. How about pizza? We could order in or go out."

"Are you sure you're not sick of me yet?" she asked with a smile.

"I'm sure. In or out?"

"Well, I'd love to say in, but if we go out, after we eat, I could go on back to your mother's house. I still have those contracts to look over for work tomorrow."

"Sounds good. Give me a few minutes to feed the cats and Murph and to change my shirt, then we can head out. Can I get you anything? A cold drink?"

"No, I'm fine, thanks. I'll wait for you then we can leave at the same time. Where are we going for the pizza?"

"Down by the rotary, do you know where I mean?"

"I think so, but I'll follow you anyway."

They sat in a booth and ordered a large veggie pizza and a pitcher of beer. The place smelled wonderful with the aroma of basil and tomato sauce, and the interior stone walls were evidence that someone had put some extra thought into the design of the building.

"I like it here," she said as the waitress placed two frosty glasses and a pitcher of beer in the center of their table.

"Yeah, me too. I come here to play pool sometimes with an old classmate. He's married with five kids: three sons and a set of twin girls. They're cute, but man, they never stop," Cole laughed.

"That could be you someday," Jerica teased.

"Could be," he said.

At the bar, just twenty feet away, loud laughter caused them to look toward the noise. Cole looked back at Jerica and found her face stone still, her eyes wide.

"What's the matter?" he asked.

Jerica was quiet at first, then she said, "That's Dan."

Cole turned to look. There were two men and two women, obviously enjoying one another's company. As they watched, one of the men, a blond-haired man in a bright red shirt, noticed Jerica and

Cole together. He stopped, left his drink on the bar and walked over to them.

"Jerica," he began. He glanced toward Cole then back at Jerica. "What are you doing here?"

She smiled, but it looked forced. "Having pizza, what about you?"

"Oh, having a few drinks, that's all. Glen and I met these two girls while rafting. They were from the area, so we invited them for a drink. I was going to call you."

Jerica nodded. "Well, now you don't have to. Cole, this is Dan. Dan, this is Cole, Mary McGinnis' son."

The two men shook hands, but Cole didn't stand.

"Well, when you're ready, I'll drive you home," Dan said.

"That's all right. I have my own car here. I have those contracts to finish up for work, so I'll be leaving soon. Why don't you give me a call later?"

"Well, yeah, I will, but just now, I need, you know..." Dan gestured toward Glen and the girls at the bar. In a moment, he walked away saying he'd call her in an hour or two.

Cole shifted in his seat.

Jerica watched Dan walk back to the bar where an attractive, athletic looking young woman with short red hair allowed her hand to rest on his shoulder. Dabbing the corners of her mouth with a napkin, Jerica gathered her purse and car keys together. "I should go," she said to Cole. "I've been procrastinating about one contract in particular, and I need to get that report done and off my mind." She looked at her companion across the table from her and smiled. "You're wonderful, Cole. I've had such a good time with you today. Thanks so much for everything."

Cole stood as she prepared to leave. He left cash on the table to cover the bill and a nice tip then he walked with Jerica to her car. It was clear Dan was too busy to notice that his beautiful girlfriend was walking away, escorted by another man.

When she had unlocked her car, Cole opened the door. She hesitated, almost as if she might lean forward with a kiss, a hug, something, but then she slid into the car and started the engine.

"Thanks again," she said.

"I'm the one who needs to do the thanking here. I've got leftover pancakes."

Jerica smiled. "Heat them in the microwave for about one minute, maybe less."

"Okay, Boss," he said, and then she was gone.

Cole walked back to his car and drove slowly home. Inside, greeted by Murphy and one of the cats, he sank into a kitchen rocking chair and wondered why it all felt so out of balance without Jerica. The answer was painfully obvious - he was in love with an unavailable woman.

At nine that evening, the phone rang and Cole answered it to hear his mother's voice. "Hi, Honey."

"Hi, Mom. How'd things go today with Deena?"

"Oh, she's ok. That knee is going to be a problem for a while, but nothing major. I was glad to be able to spend part of the day with her. I hope you didn't mind too much. I thought you and Jerica would enjoy one another's company anyway."

"Yes, we did. It was nice. You missed the French Pancakes, but I'll bet Jerica would make them for you, or maybe I could make them for you. She taught me how."

Mary McGinnis laughed. "I'll get some from one of you soon. Were they good?"

"Better than good."

Mary smiled, "And the day with Jerica was pleasant?"

"Yup. It was all good. Is she home?"

"Oh, yes. She came in, took a shower, and went to her room to work. What a nice girl she is. Twenty-four and so put together."

"I noticed," he said.

Mary laughed. "Yes, but maybe you noticed her being put together in a different manner? She's a beautiful girl."

"I noticed it all, Mom. Anyway, I'm glad things are okay with you – things are okay with me too, so maybe we could do dinner one night this week. I'll barbeque if you'd like."

"Are you kidding? I'd love it. I can make vegetable shish-ka-bobs for us too. I have some wonderful fresh peppers and tomatoes. I can add mushrooms and onions, maybe even some breaded zucchini. How about Jerica? Okay if I tell her about this and invite her along?"

Cole closed his eyes for a moment then said, "Sure, why not." Deeper and deeper, that's where this whole thing is going. Will I be able to dig my way out? He wondered. He didn't want to. He wanted to pull her into the place where he was, but only if she wanted to be there and not with Dan.

Chapter Three

Cole purposely allowed a few days to pass without extending the barbeque invitation to his mother and Jerica. It was Mary who called to check in and then Cole felt he couldn't escape mentioning having them over.

"I'm fine, Mom," he said. "The last sailing class is coming up - these kids are older, teens, so there's a little more to it. But, I'm ready to barbeque anytime you're up for it."

"That sounds very appealing," Mary McGinnis said. "What's tomorrow evening like for you? I've got some wonderful vegetables ready to roast."

Cole stood in his kitchen, the phone in one hand, rubbing his brow with the other. "Okay, tomorrow's good. I'll be in from sailing by three, so that'll give me some prep time. Would around six work for you?"

"Perfect," Mary said. "You take charge of the barbeque. I'll make some things to go with it."

When the conversation was over, Cole put the phone back onto its receiver and leaned against his counter. He was wondering how the future was going to play itself out with Jerica. He felt it could be a dead end. As he pondered how to handle things with her, Murphy came along and stood next to him, wagging his tail slowly.

"Hey, Murph," Cole spoke to the dog. "Come on, I'll get your supper. I suppose those whiskered friends of yours are hungry too."

When Cole had set out fresh bowls of water and food for his pets, he took a cold drink from the refrigerator and walked out onto his patio to sit in the shade. He couldn't wait for tomorrow evening and yet he dreaded it. Jerica was a fantastic girl, the kind he'd dreamed of.

The next evening, just after six, Cole's mother walked into his kitchen with a large basket on one arm.

"What have you got there? Looks like you brought the grocery store," Cole said. Then he looked around Mary for Jerica. His heart lurched when he didn't see her.

"I didn't buy out anything," Mary said. "This is from my own garden and kitchen."

"Great," he said as he helped remove vegetables and potato salad from the basket. "Where's Jerica?" He tried not to seem too interested.

"Oh, she's coming. She wanted to stop by the bakery for something sweet to add to our meal. She's such a delight."

Cole couldn't tell if his rapid heartbeat was due to Jerica's absence or the promise that she would be there. He made small talk with his mother while she sliced vegetables and he prepared his contribution for the barbeque. As he turned to toss a Frisbee to Murphy, Jerica appeared and ducked.

"Was that aimed at me" she asked with a smile.

Cole laughed. "Well, at least not while you're carrying that box from the bakery. What did you buy for me?"

Jerica raised her eyebrows and gave him a stern look. "What did I buy for you?"

Cole smiled and shrugged.

"What can I do to help?" she asked.

"I'm all set out here," he said. "Maybe you could check with Mom, she's in the kitchen. Oh, I didn't make anything to drink. Maybe you could make some iced tea, unless you and Mom are good with soda or beer, I've got that all cold."

"I'll check with your mother," Jerica said as she brushed past him and walked into his kitchen.

The three of them had become comfortable together, almost too good to be true. After the meal had been enjoyed, Mary excused herself saying that she wanted to stop over to visit Deena. "I hope you two don't mind," she said, "I feel so bad for her. That knee is going to require surgery after all. It's swollen and painful. I'll see you at home, Jerica, and Cole: good barbeque." She leaned forward to hug her son. "Thanks, Honey, it was a treat."

"Your ka-bobs gave it the colorful boost," he said hugging her. "Say hi to Deena for me."

He walked his mother out to the patio then rejoined Jerica as she tidied up his kitchen.

"I should probably go too," she said.

"More reports to work on?" he asked.

"No, I've actually caught up," she said while slipping into Cole's kitchen rocking chair. "I like this chair, and I like that it's in your kitchen."

Cole smiled and sat down across from her at his kitchen table. "That was my grandmother's. She had it in her kitchen. I remember her sitting in it snapping the ends off green beans."

"Nice memory," Jerica said.

"What's happening with your family? Have they decided to move back here?"

Jerica shook her head from side to side. "It's hard really. My sister lives in Ohio with her husband and baby daughter, and my brother is still in college out there. They love New England, especially the Mystic area, but it's been twenty-two years, and they're very rooted there."

"How's all this affecting you? Wasn't there an expectation for them to follow you out here?"

Jerica rocked in the old chair and nodded. "Yes, but, well I don't know. I came out here for several reasons."

Cole knew that one of those reasons was Dan.

"Can I get you a cold drink? We could sit out on the patio, or we can stay here, whatever your heart desires," he said with a smile. She was not with Dan tonight, she was here and he was going to enjoy it.

"You know, I'd love a cup of hot tea, and I'd really like to stay in this rocker as long as you're comfortable."

Cole stood to pour water into a cup and then placed it in the microwave, a teabag ready. "Milk? Sugar?" he asked.

"Plain," she said.

"Okay, that'll be ready in about two minutes. I'm going out on the patio to grab a comfy chair, I'll be right back."

When he came back into the kitchen, he placed his chair facing Jerica's; then finished fixing her tea. He took a bottle of water from the refrigerator for himself.

"I love this," Jerica said.

Cole smiled. "We're like two old fuddy-duddies. Really live wires."

Jerica laughed then took a sip of her hot tea. "What kinds of things do you like to do for fun?" she asked.

"For fun. Let me think. I like to sail, I enjoy a good book, I like some TV, I have a good time with Murph. The cats aren't interested in my state of mind, but I like them anyway. I figure their attitude is good training if I ever have a wife."

Jerica laughed. "That's a terrible thing to say."

"Okay, what about you? What do you do for enjoyment?"

She sipped more of her tea, holding the warm mug in her hands. "I like lots of things: movies, books, walks in pretty places, baking, eating what I bake." She smiled. "And there used to be pets. We had this really cute dog, Swifty, and a black and white cat, Nola. I loved them so much."

"What happened with them?" Cole asked, half afraid the answer would upset her.

"Swifty lived to be seventeen, Nola nineteen. I hated losing them, but I knew we'd been lucky to have had them so long. When they died, Mom talked about another pet, but it never happened. I think their loss was too hard for her. So, it's nice to be around your pets. I've wondered why your mother doesn't have a cat or a dog, but I haven't asked."

Cole grimaced a bit. "I think for the same reason your mother doesn't. Mom always had a cat. After the last one, I don't know, I think that was all she could take. Dad died the year before the cat; it was a bad time."

Jerica nodded. "Maybe someday," she said, "some needy little thing will find its way to her and she'll take it in as she did me."

"That's possible."

31

Jerica closed her eyes and rocked slowly, careful not to spill her tea.

"When you were little, did you really fall in love with me?" she asked with a slight smile on her lips. "Your mother told me you were inconsolable when my family moved away."

Cole looked at her beautiful face, cherishing the opportunity to scan every detail while her eyes were closed. And then she opened them and they were both surprised, locked in a visual embrace.

"I was seven," Cole said. "I thought you'd live next door forever. I remember feeling so helpless when I was told you were gone."

"No one said anything to you before we actually left?"

Cole shook his head from side to side. "No. They might have been afraid to tell me, or maybe they didn't know I'd be so upset. It was my first loss - I guess that was part of it."

Jerica smiled. Cole was a tall, sturdy looking man, incredibly handsome. She was picturing him as a little boy, sad over losing her from his life.

"I don't know if grown ups fully understand how little control they offer to their children," she said. "After we moved to Ohio, we lived in one house for almost nine years. Then, suddenly, we were packing and told that we were moving to a town a few miles away. For us, my sister who was seven, my brother four, and me at nine, it was a huge adjustment. My sister and I were subjected to new schools, new friends, loss of old friends and the familiarity of our home. And it was hard for my brother too. He lost his neighborhood playmates. I know they didn't mean for us to suffer from the move," she continued. "It was a bigger house and all, but we did suffer."

Cole took a drink from his water bottle. "Yeah, I think you're right. Maybe parents don't think kids will find the adjustment hard when changes are made. I was lucky to have both my parents for so long and to grow up in the same house where my mother still lives."

Jerica nodded and then they were quiet. The sky was turning dark as Cole decided that Murphy needed one more visit outside. "I'll be right back," he said.

Jerica used that time to stand and move to the sink where she washed her tea mug. Then she took her purse and car keys and walked out onto the patio.

Cole hadn't heard her and in the dark as he directed Murphy inside with him, he bumped into Jerica.

"Jerica, I'm sorry, I didn't realize you were there."

Their eyes reflected a luminous moon; their lips were still, until they met. When they'd released one another, it felt awkward but right. Neither of them apologized.

"Thanks for tonight," she said as she walked toward her car.

Cole stood and watched the lights of the car go on, then he regretted seeing the two red tail lights as she drove away. He walked Murphy back into the kitchen, locked the door, and touched the arm of the rocker. The house felt empty now. That night, Cole tried to sleep, but thoughts of her kept him awake.

Jerica lay in her bed and stared at the moon through her window, then touched a forefinger to her lips, tracing the kiss.

Chapter Four

The next morning was Friday and Jerica enjoyed lingering in her comfortable bed, the one Cole had slept in for most of his life. One more day at work, and then there were possibilities for the weekend. She thought of Cole. He was incredible, but she felt him keeping his distance. He could have wrapped himself around her last night during that spontaneous kiss, but he'd let go. What was that all about? She thought about Dan. He'd been so busy lately, she wondered if she could lure him away to someplace where they could relax, have some fun, and maybe swim. She hadn't been swimming all summer, and having grown up with a pool, she missed that connection to the water. Her thoughts returned to Dan. She wondered what their future entailed. He'd asked her to marry him twice, and twice she'd laughed and told him they'd talk about it later. Now she wondered if she'd been subconsciously discouraging him all along. She didn't know, but they'd been together for more than four years; she felt the relationship deserved a try. She would call him later in the day and suggest a weekend getaway.

Cole had risen early and made a fresh pot of coffee. He hadn't slept well with thoughts of Jerica dancing around in his head. He ran his hand through his dark hair as he stood at the kitchen window waiting for the coffee and watching Murphy explore the back yard. When the coffee was ready, he poured some into a white porcelain mug and sat down at the table to review the sailing charts for the day.

This was it, the end of the classes and he was glad. Now he had two weeks of free time before school opened and he'd be back in front of the blackboard.

Murphy scratched at the screen door. Cole walked the few steps to where he invited the agreeable dog to come back in. The three cats were munching on some people tuna fish and dry kibble, keeping an eye on Murphy who they knew would be happy to clean up their leftovers.

Cole sat down again and slid back in his chair, a quick glance at the rocker. He could sit there; he had better than an hour before he'd need to leave for the docks, but something told him no, that's Jerica's chair. In the pit of his stomach, he felt a sense of fear that he could very well lose her again. She wasn't his; she never was, except in his heart.

"Jerica," Mary McGinnis said as the younger woman bustled into the kitchen, her purse and car keys in her hands. "Where are you off to in such a hurry? No breakfast?"

Jerica smiled. "Just like home. No, I'll grab a tea and muffin at the hospital cafeteria. I'm hoping to get in early and out early. I'm going to try talking Dan into a weekend away."

"Oh," Mary said as she swallowed a sip of coffee. "That sounds nice." But inside, she was thinking, poor Cole. "Any special occasion?"

"No, it's just that we seem to have disconnected a bit. This job I have is so involved, and Dan's work has him in a race too. I think we need a break."

Mary nodded. "You might be right," she said, but she didn't think so and she certainly didn't want to think so. Although biased, she deeply felt that no better match could be found for Cole and Jerica than in one another.

Later in the afternoon, Jerica phoned Mary to say that she would be leaving directly from work. She and Dan were going from Hartford to Stamford to see his family. Mary sat for a good fifteen minutes thinking about the situation. She was certain that Jerica was making the wrong move, but, then, no one asked for her opinion on the matter.

She thought of Cole and decided she'd do her best to keep him occupied.

At four, when she knew he'd be home from sailing class, she called him. "Hi Honey, how'd the last class go? Are you glad it's over for the summer?"

"I am," he said. "I had a good group of kids, but it's the repetitiveness of it I think. I'm not sure I'll do this anymore."

"Really?" Mary asked. "Gee, you've been giving sailing lessons since you were fourteen. Can't imagine you not doing it."

Cole opened cans of cat food for his cats and then a can of dog food for Murphy, all while he spoke to his mother.

"I'll always love sailing; I'm just not that enthused about doing classes. We'll see. I need to get back to school too. Teaching at the college level might be interesting."

"Yes," Mary McGinnis said, "I always thought you'd end up teaching college. I think you'd be good at it, Professor McGinnis."

Cole laughed. "It has a nice ring to it," he said.

"So," she began, "what are you up to this weekend?"

"That's a good question. Jerica indicated that she'd like to go sailing sometime. I thought I might take her out for a couple of hours tomorrow if she hasn't made plans."

Mary bit her lower lip then said, "She's gone for the weekend, Honey, leaving from work."

"Oh," Cole replied, his heart feeling pummeled. "Well, I guess that's that. I have lots of things to do here; I'll keep busy. What about you? Any plans? Maybe we could see a movie tomorrow night, grab a bite to eat out."

"Listen," she said, "I think you know that I love spending time with you, but you need friends your own age. Don't you know any nice girls you could ask out?"

Cole smiled. Yeah, he knew Jerica, but apparently that wasn't going to work. "I don't know, Mom. I'm either too fussy or there's too few available women in the area. One of these days, someone will show up, I'm sure. In the meantime, I've got you!"

"All right," Mary said, "if nothing else comes your way, we could do pizza and a movie tomorrow night. Tonight I'm taking a salad and rolls to Deena's, and I'll visit with her for a bit. And Sunday, Jim has asked me to accompany him to a garden wedding, a small affair. His cousin, a widow, is marrying for the second time. Better her than me!"

Cole laughed. "What? No more walking down the aisle for you?"

"Oh, my goodness, no!" she said.

"How come? Maybe you haven't met the right person."

"Yes, I did," she said, "thirty-two years ago. That's enough. I'm not going to train another one!"

Cole laughed again. "I see. So what's going on with Jim? I know he's interested."

"Yes, well, I know that too. And I like Jim, but no, I don't want to marry him and I'm not misleading him. An occasional date is nice enough."

"Ok," Cole said, "I think we've got that subject covered. Now, how about if we plan on tomorrow night then? Maybe I'll venture out for a game of pool tonight while you visit Deena. Give her my best."

They chatted for a few more minutes then Cole sank into a chair on his patio, closed his eyes and rubbed Murphy's ears. Two full hours passed before he opened his eyes and realized he'd been sleeping soundly. A wind had kicked up and the sky was gray with cumbersome clouds sprinkling a light mist and offering a threat of hard rain. "Come on inside, Murph. Maybe this is one of those nights when I'll stay in with you and the cats. We'll buckle ourselves up for the night with a good book."

Back inside, Cole made himself a sandwich, took a cold drink from the refrigerator, ran around closing windows against the now pouring rain, then sat down in his recliner with his supper. This house needs a woman, he thought, then immediately felt a case of the blues knowing that there was only Jerica on his mind.

He tore down some old molding in the dining room and started putting up crown molding in its place. By ten-thirty, he was tired but ready for something else to eat. The rain had stopped and he opened a few windows, inviting the sweet, salty air inside. He gave Murphy a pat on the head, said he'd be back soon, then took his wallet and car keys and left locking the door behind him.

The pizza place at the rotary was jumping. He could smell the pizza and beer from outside, and he could hear the boisterous laughter. This was what he needed, signs of life.

He walked over to the bar and ordered a cheese pizza and a cold beer. Within moments, a fellow teacher from the high school walked over to greet him.

"Hey, Cole," he said, "haven't seen you all summer. What's happening? Did you teach sailing again this year?"

"Yeah, I did. How about you, Ken? How's Lizzy?"

"Lizzy's fine, she's over at the table, come and join us. In fact, her cousin's here visiting from Georgia. Come and meet her."

"Sure, let me grab my pizza and I'll be right over with you," Cole said, thinking how everyone was anxious to fix him up with someone. The pizza arrived and Cole took it over to where Ken, Lizzy, and an attractive brunette sat. Ken made the introductions and everyone sat down.

"Anyone want some of this pizza?" Cole asked.

"We ate already," Lizzy said. "We stuffed ourselves, right Kathy?"

Kathy smiled at Cole. "We did, but it was worth it. The pizza here is so good."

Ken and Lizzy made light conversation with Cole while he ate half of the pizza, then he looked at Kathy who seemed content to take it all in. "So, you're here on vacation?" he asked.

Kathy poked Lizzy and smiled. "I wouldn't call it a vacation, would you, Lizzy?"

Lizzy laughed. "Well, you're enjoying yourself tonight, aren't you?"

Kathy looked at Cole then explained. "I came to visit my parents. They're very mad at me for moving to Georgia. I've been there for six years, but they're still mad. Lizzy and Ken rescued me tonight, and thank goodness, just three more days and then I'm back in Atlanta."

Cole nodded, but he thought how fortunate he was to have the mother he had, someone with whom he enjoyed spending time.

"Cole," Lizzy began, "maybe you'd like to join us tomorrow evening. Ken and I are having a family cook-out; you could be Kathy's date."

"Oh, that sounds wonderful," Kathy said. "Can you make it, Cole?"

He looked from one to the other and he thought it might be interesting - Kathy wasn't hard to look at, but he'd made plans with his mother and he wasn't breaking them. "It sounds like fun," he said, "but I can't, I'm sorry."

Kathy looked disappointed.

"Will you be around on Sunday?" he asked. "Weather permitting, we could go out for a little sail."

Her face brightened. "I'd love that," she said. "I used to sail all the time when I lived here. Thanks."

"Around noon okay?" he asked.

"Sure," Kathy replied, and the plans were made.

When Sunday came, Cole went through all the same steps he did each day, feeding Murphy and letting him out into the fenced yard. He fed the cats, cleaned their litter boxes, showered and shaved, then drank a cup of black coffee. He wondered while doing all the familiar tasks why he'd made these plans with Kathy. She was pretty and she was nice enough, but she wasn't Jerica. Then he had his answer. He needed the Kathys of the world to help him through the Jericas of the world. He would show up at noon for Kathy and they would have a good time. Before leaving, Cole called his mother to check in.

"You all set for the wedding?" he asked.

"I think so. I've tried on three different outfits, finally decided on the tan suit with my amber jewelry. What are you up to today?"

Cole smiled and looked outside at the pale blue sky and puffy white clouds. "I actually have a date to go sailing," he said, knowing that his mother would be pleased.

"A date? With whom?"

"She's Lizzy's cousin, up from Georgia. She used to live here, Kathy Bezanson."

"Hmm," Mary began, "Bezanson. I don't think I know anyone by that name. So, she's nice?"

Cole laughed. "Yes, Mom, she's nice, and she's pretty, and don't forget, she's visiting from Georgia. So don't make any wedding plans for me just yet."

Mary laughed. "You're too much. Well, I'm glad you're not alone today, Honey. I hope you and this Kathy have fun."

When Mary placed the phone back on its receiver, she lingered there for a few minutes. She so loved this son of hers, and she wanted him to be with someone, as long as it was the right someone.

At ten o'clock Sunday evening, Jerica arrived back in Mystic. She unlocked the door and walked into Mary's kitchen where she found a note explaining the older woman's absence. Jerica turned on lights as she made her way upstairs until she got to the upstairs hallway where the lights, none of them, would go on. She went back downstairs and decided to call Cole - maybe he could tell her how to rectify the situation. She dialed the number, it rang, and then a woman answered. Jerica felt like the phone was on fire, burning her hand. She put it down and walked backward a few steps to a comfortable chair.

"Was that the phone?" Cole asked as he walked back in to the room.

"Yes. Whoever it was hung up. Hope I didn't upset a prospective girlfriend," Kathy teased.

"How about that drink I promised you? Or would you prefer coffee, tea, or soda?"

"I'd love a glass of wine if you have it," she said, her long legs curled beneath her on the sofa.

"Sure. Rose, merlot, or pinot grigio? That's my stock right now."

"Perfect. I'll have the Merlot, thank you."

Cole poured two glasses of wine in stemware from his grandmother's collection.

"I've had such a great day, Cole. Thank you for everything," she said and then she sipped the dark wine.

"You're welcome. I had a good time too."

Kathy looked at him and wondered how a man who looked and behaved this good, who was intelligent and sweet, had managed to stay single.

"You're really kind of a dinosaur," she said.

Cole laughed. "Thanks, I think."

"No, I mean that in a good way," she said. "You're really amazing, with this old house and all. Care to move down to Atlanta?"

Cole smiled. "How did a Mystic girl end up in Georgia anyway?"

"Escaping, I guess. I have a very strict, domineering set of parents, and after college, I'd decided to let go of the boyfriend they thought I'd settle down with. The job opportunity came along for Atlanta, I needed the breathing room, and besides, it's great down there. I have a nice condo, everything fits. It's a place where life happens."

Cole nodded and finished his wine. For him, Mystic was that place, where life happened. His kiss goodnight to her was light and expected. He could have, and should have, enjoyed it more. Kathy was the kind of woman most men would be thrilled to have in their lives. But she simply wasn't Jerica.

Chapter Five

Monday morning Mary thought Jerica was a bit subdued. She didn't want her usual tea, nothing to eat, she just wanted to run off to work, no word about how the weekend at Dan's family home went.

As Mary stirred a bit of cream into her coffee, the phone rang and it was Cole.

"Hi, Mom. How was the wedding? Jim stay over night?" he teased.

"You stop that!" she said smiling. "Jim's home where Jim belongs."

Cole laughed. "Okay. So, how was the wedding? You had a nice day for it."

"Yes, it was nice. I'd say there were eighty or so people there. The garden was very pretty, lots of roses everywhere, and people were friendly. Poor Jerica though, when I got home at eleven, she was sitting in the kitchen instead of upstairs in her own rooms. The lights up there were out. I went down cellar to the circuit box, and sure enough, just a flip of the switch made everything right again."

"Oh. I'm surprised she didn't give me a call to see if I could help."

"I asked her about that. She said she didn't want to bother you."

But then, there had been that call Kathy answered, where the caller had hung up. Jerica? he wondered. Well, even if it was, she was with Dan for the weekend, so what would it matter if the call was from her. He thought about it for a few minutes and realized more so than ever, he didn't want to do anything to trouble Jerica, Dan or no Dan.

At work, Jerica fumbled with her copy machine, then she pressed a few keys on her computer to bring up files she needed for a morning presentation to the hospital finance committee. After a few more fumbles, she stopped, took a deep breath, then decided she needed her tea. In the cafeteria, bustling with doctors, nurses, administrative people, and visitors, she found an available table and sat down with her steaming brew. She looked out the second story window and could see the center of town and a slice of deep green sea. A sailboat caught her eyes and she watched as it slid smoothly among other anchored boats and then out of view.

This wasn't the job she wanted. This was the place she wanted and she loved the people, but administrative work was not for her.

No matter how hard she tried, she couldn't get that silky female voice from last night out of her mind. Cole. Why would she think he wouldn't have someone? He represented everything she could dream of in a man, and maybe because she wasn't so sure she deserved that, it did not occur to her that she should try for him. And there was Dan, accessible Dan, who insisted he loved her, wanted her, needed her. She thought too of his family. His parents were wealthy, pleasant, but there was that embarrassing mention of Laura, Dan's former girlfriend. Jerica found it both interesting and annoying that her name was mentioned so easily in front of her. Shouldn't thoughts of former girlfriends who are back in town be kept under wrap?

Jerica sipped her tea, then stood and took it with her back to the office where she continued preparations for her meeting. She started by entering information into her computer, but after about twenty minutes, she sat back, took a swallow of tea, then stared at a black and white screen showing statistics and explanations for staff expenses. Her eyes were seeing something different - reflections of her feelings for Cole. Why couldn't she get him out of her mind? She stood and walked around her small office, stopping to look out the window over the parking lot, eye-level with the green treetops. She wondered what dose of fate brought her here to this opening at St. Joseph's Hospital, to this magical seaport where Cole McGinnis lived his entire life. Fate? Mistake? She didn't know. She sat down at the computer and went back to work.

As Cole thought about the last couple of weeks before school began, he decided that maybe he needed a few days away. Kathy was returning to Georgia in another day. He'd ask her out to dinner, and then he'd see about a mini vacation. Receptive to his invitation to dinner, Kathy wore a revealing burgundy dress with strappy sandals in the same color. There was no doubt about it, she was enticing.

"So, what's on your agenda for the remainder of the summer?" she asked. "You know, it was a genuine invitation when I asked you about coming down to Georgia."

Cole smiled, turning his stemmed wine glass in his left hand. "Thank you. I just might do that sometime, but something tells me it can get pretty warm in Georgia this time of year."

"It can, but everything's air conditioned. I keep my condo nice and cool to the point that I sleep with a blanket at night."

Cole looked at her and found a bit of mischief and allure in Kathy's eyes.

"I'll keep that in mind," he said. But his destination would not be Georgia this time around. He thought of a day or two in Boston to see some old college friends and then a couple of days in New Hampshire. Murphy could go with him or stay with the cats. He knew that his mother would be more than willing to pet sit. He would ask her about it in the morning, after Kathy was tucked on her flight back to Georgia.

Cole's mother was pleased to hear her son planning to get away for a few days. Between working on his house and teaching sailing, she felt he needed the change, and maybe from Jerica as well.

"You'll have nothing to worry about," Mary said. "Go and have a good time. And leave Murphy. Some hotels and motels aren't that animal friendly, and he loves his own home. I'll stay there with your crew if need be, don't give it another thought."

Cole made his plans and early on Thursday morning, after assuring Murphy and the cats he'd be back soon, he drove to Boston, expecting to return the following Tuesday. He felt sorry to leave, he loved home, but he needed a diversion.

When Jerica was leaving for work that morning, Mary told her that she would be going over to Cole's to take care of the pets. She'd probably be home to sleep, most likely with Murphy in tow.

Jerica felt a pang of loneliness that he was gone. No one had mentioned that he might go away for a few days, and Tuesday felt like a lifetime away. That depressed feeling stayed with her all day at work and, angry with herself for caring so much, she treated herself to a cup of hot chocolate and drank it all in the cafeteria rather than back at her desk.

That evening, she made herself a sandwich and took it upstairs to her room where she spoke with Dan on the phone, worked on her laptop, and read. When she heard Mary come in, Jerica went downstairs in her pajamas and slippers. Murphy greeted her by wagging his slightly curled tail. Jerica took his ears in her hands and leaned over to kiss the top of his head.

"Did you eat, Mary?" she asked. "I had a sandwich. I could make one for you."

"Thank you, Dear," Mary said as she hung Murphy's leash over the back of a kitchen chair. "I've had all I need for now. Cole had leftovers he told me to use, so I did. Maybe I'll have a cold drink later."

Jerica moved to sit down at the kitchen table where she could better pat Murphy. "Is he staying with us tonight?"

Mary laughed. "We'll see. If he's content, yes. If not, I'll take him back around ten, that's usually when Cole takes him out for his bedtime walk."

Jerica nodded and then gave her full attention to the dog, talking to him, smoothing his sleek coat along his neck and back.

"You like this funny old pooch, don't you?" Mary said.

"What's not to like? I love Murph. How old is he anyway?"

"Oh, he's a pup comparatively speaking. Murph came from a local shelter; he's only two or three."

"He's so gentle, I would have thought him to be older."

"He's gentle and smart," Mary began. "He knows the cats are the bosses. Poor dog, they walk under his belly when he's trying to eat."

Jerica laughed. "Now that's what I call a gentleman."

Mary smiled. "He's that all right. Just like his pal."

Jerica understood that Mary meant Cole, but the very thought of him made her heart race. She stood and reluctantly said that she should go back upstairs to do some work. In truth, she had finished her work and she would read.

At ten o'clock, Mary hollered up the stairs to Jerica. "I'm taking Murph home. He's acting anxious. I think he misses those cats. I'll stay there tonight. Will you be okay here on your own?"

"Sure," Jerica said from the top of the stairs. "Would you prefer that I go? I don't mind at all."

"Oh, heavens, no. I'll go. Maybe you could do Saturday night there if you have no plans. I've been invited to a ceremonial dinner and I could be late getting in. We'll see. We can work something out if you can't."

"No, Saturday night would be fine, Mary. Dan is going to New York to a bachelor party. I'll be on my own."

Mary looked at the younger woman. Jerica had a smile on her pretty face, but there was a glimmer of sadness too.

"Is everything okay, Jerica? You seem a little, I don't know, down. Are you feeling all right?"

"I'm fine. A little on the weary side, that's all."

"How's work been?" Mary asked.

Jerica shrugged her shoulders then walked down the stairs to stroke Murphy. "It's not terrible or anything, it's just so intricate and boring at the same time. It isn't what I want to do for a career, but I didn't realize that until I started working. My parents aren't going to be happy with me when I finally tell them I made this huge mistake."

Mary gave her a thoughtful look. "I think they'll understand, Dear. I remember your folks as being sweet, calm people."

"They are, but it was an expense sending me to college. I really should have thought things out better than I did."

"It'll work out, you'll see. Now, I'm taking Murphy home, are you really okay with being here alone tonight? You can come with me if you wish. I thought I'd come back here in the morning after everyone's settled. Murph is used to being on his own during the day while Cole teaches, so I'll try to keep the routine the same."

"I'm fine, Mary, and count on me for Saturday night. I'd enjoy sitting for Murphy and the cats, and actually, I'll have a chance to enjoy Cole's home too. It will be fun."

"That sounds good," Mary said. "The dinner isn't that important to me, so if you change your mind about Saturday night, there's no problem."

Jerica hooked Murphy's leash to his collar. "I'm sure it'll be fine. You go along with this handsome fellow. I'll see you tomorrow."

Mary hugged Jerica lightly and told her to lock up, then she was gone.

Jerica sat for a few minutes and then shut off the bright lights, leaving dimmed lights to keep the house from being dark. She hesitated at the stairway and decided to sleep on the family room sofa rather than upstairs in bed. She wrapped herself in a soft blue and white afghan and looked around the room. There were framed photos of Cole as an infant, a child, a teenager and an adult, and there were photos of Mary with Cole's father. It was a room filled with warmth, with memories and love. Jerica thought of her own family so far away in Ohio. Although there were family members in and near Connecticut, they weren't emotionally close. Growing up in Ohio had separated the families to the point that, in their absence, they had all filled in with other relationships. She glanced at a photo of Cole when he was about four, his legs straddling a bike with training wheels, his father smiling proudly at his side. She sighed, closed her eyes, and went to sleep.

Chapter Six

On Saturday morning, Cole left Boston after visiting his friends and spending time at their favorite hangouts. Sitting in Harvard Square with a cup of coffee at a sunny outside café table, he recalled the free-wheeling, exciting college years, filled with late night pizzas and last minute preparations for tests. It had been fun, but there were only a few friends left in the area and, other than himself, they were all attached: either dating someone or married with kids. Peaceful, relaxing New Hampshire would be a welcome change.

After the two-hour drive north, Cole pulled up to a motel where he'd made reservations. When he stepped out of the car, he stretched and noticed the refreshing, crisp mountain air. He thought about Murphy. He wouldn't have enjoyed Boston, but he'd love this place. As nice as it was to get away, Cole felt he'd be ready to head home on Tuesday morning. He'd call his mother later just to say hi and check on things. Then he wondered what Jerica was doing. The weekend - she was probably with Dan. Cole shook his head; he really didn't like that guy. Seeing him living it up with those girls at the bar in the pizza place that day, he wanted to sock him one. Jerica deserved better.

Mary McGinnis woke up at Cole's, the three cats and Murphy all on her bed. She laughed as she pet each one of them. "You guys really take advantage of Grandma, don't you?" She pushed the covers aside, remade the bed, then went downstairs to let Murphy out and to fix breakfast for all of them. She started to make coffee but decided she'd wait until she got home. She changed from her nightgown into casual slacks and a pale blue sweater, slipping the slippers off and her loafers on. With Murphy in tow, she left Cole's house, leaving ceiling fans on for the cats, and drove home. The guest room bed was ok, but she'd look forward to sleeping in her own comfortable bed tonight, as long as Jerica could still stay with Cole's pets.

In her kitchen she found Jerica reading the paper while sipping tea, but she could smell the sweet aroma of freshly brewed coffee. The young woman looked up and smiled.

"Hi Mary, welcome home, and you too, Murphy. I made coffee, and there are cranberry-pecan scones from the bakery."

Murphy wagged his tail - those scones held the promise for an interesting nibble.

"Well," Mary said, "this is a treat, isn't it Murphy? Thank you, Dear, I'm longing for a good cup of coffee, and I'll share a scone with my fuzzy friend here. Did you sleep all right last night? I felt so bad leaving you on your own."

"Don't give it another thought, Mary. I've been fine. So, tonight's my night, right?"

Mary poured coffee into a cup and added a splash of cream. "If you're certain you don't mind. I'm not that interested in this dinner tonight, I can easily skip it."

"No," Jerica insisted, "you go, Mary. It will be fun, you'll see. And besides, I'm looking forward to being at Cole's place. I really love it there."

Mary smiled at Jerica. "Well, be prepared for four lazy creatures to join you in bed. It's lucky none of them snores."

Jerica laughed. "I'm sure I'll manage fine."

That evening, Mary went off with Jim to the dinner and Jerica took Murphy home where they could settle in for the night. Once there, she let Murphy wander the fenced backyard while she fed the cats. They watched her, almost enchanted with her sprightly moves and her gentle voice speaking to them. She opened food for Murphy, then made herself a glass of iced tea to go with a salad she'd made earlier in the day. With Murphy back inside, she sat in the kitchen rocking chair and ate as she looked around. Both mother and son had a knack for creating a warm home. It was then that she noticed the long, romantic sign over Cole's back door quoting part of an old poem, "A tall ship and a star to steer her by." Jerica felt very fortunate to be living with Mary and to have this chance to further enjoy Cole's place too. Cole. She missed him. Knowing he was so far off made her feel sad, but she also regretted that she felt that way. Obviously he had women friends, and she had to think about Dan.

Before dark, she let Murphy out again for a few minutes then decided to look among Cole's bookshelves for something to read. After scanning a few pages of Time of Peace by Ben Ames Williams, she decided that was her type of book. She went to the door barefoot and called Murphy inside. Together, the three cats, the dog, and Jerica, settled in for a wonderfully quiet evening.

At around nine-thirty, the phone rang and startled Jerica who was immersed in the novel.

"Is that you, Jerica?" the strong male voice asked after she'd answered with a hello.

"Yes. Cole?"

"Yeah. I tried calling Mom. When I had no answer, I figured she might be at my place."

"Oh, yes. She went to a ceremonial dinner with Jim. I hope you don't mind, I offered to stay here tonight with Murphy and the cats."

Cole felt his heart pound a little harder. "Oh, well thank you, that's nice of you. How're they doing? I suppose the cats are doing their own thing, off in one of the upstairs rooms."

Jerica smiled and was glad Cole couldn't see her. "Actually, they're all right here next to me. I've been reading."

"Really?"

"Really what? That I'm reading or that they're all here next to me?" Jerica laughed.

Cole smiled. Suddenly his motel room was a barren and lonely place. "I meant my traitorous cats. They usually disperse, hang out upstairs someplace. So, what are you reading?"

"It's one of your books: Time of Peace."

"Ah, one of my favorites."

"Un-huh. I like it very much. If I don't finish it before I go back to your mother's tomorrow, may I borrow it?"

"Sure, no problem. There's another of his there too, Come Spring."

"Ok, thanks," she said. "So, how's your vacation? Are you in New Hampshire now?"

"Yes, I am. I had a good time in Boston; saw my old college roommate and a few other friends. One of the guys who was easily the smartest of all of us is now the owner and operator of a hot dog stand. Can you believe that? This guy could have been the CEO of a big company, but no, he's running a hot dog stand, actually a few of them, and making good money doing it. It's amazing."

Jerica put her book down and smiled. "I guess if he's happy, that's what counts."

"Yeah. He's a character. He and his wife and two little boys live on the third floor of a building they own; it looks like a warehouse. The rooms they have are huge, the furnishings are warm and cozy, and the view of the city is incredible. His wife plays the flute with the symphony. She's a great girl."

"It sounds like you've been having fun."

Cole hesitated, thinking how wonderful it would have been to be with Jerica on this whole trip. "Yeah, it's been a good change."

"So, now that you're in New Hampshire, what are you doing? Do you have friends there too?"

"No, no one. My parents and I used to come up this way, to North Conway, when I was a kid. I remember going every year to see these black bears at a trading post not too far from here. That was the highlight of my New Hampshire trips. I must have at least a dozen figures of black bears packed away, souvenirs I collected from the time I was maybe four to nine or ten years old. I should dig them out of my mother's attic and put them on one of my shelves in the study. But, North Conway is just a pretty place, great skiing area, and at this time of year, a refreshing change. I'll do a little hiking, maybe swimming; there's a nice pool here where I'm staying, and other than that, I don't know, maybe I'll hit a book store later and see what looks good."

Jerica sighed thinking how easy it was to converse with him. It was relaxing, like speaking with an old and dear friend. "Sounds like a place I'd enjoy going sometime," she said.

"Yeah, I think you'd like it, and Boston too. There's so much to do there; it's culturally rich. I went to The Museum of Fine Arts and The

Isabella Stewart Gardner Museum while I was there. It had been years, since college, and I was amazed at it all. It's terrific."

Jerica smiled and stroked Edgar who sat on her lap. "We're not losing you to Boston, are we?"

Cole smiled. "No way. I love it there, but Mystic is home and that's where I'll stay. So, you're on your own tonight?"

"Yes, Dan went to New York City for a weekend bachelor party. I'm not sure I like those things. Have you ever been? I'll bet you've been to lots of them."

Cole sat down in a roomy chair by a window overlooking brightly lit cafes and other little shops and, in the background, blackish mountains against a deep blue evening sky. "I've been to a few," he said. "Mostly it's a bunch of guys getting drunk as skunks, not my idea of fun."

Jerica closed her eyes for a moment. Dan had been very excited about this party; he couldn't stop talking about going on this New York adventure.

"How's Mom?" Cole asked.

"She's great as always. She's really funny about Jim. You can tell he adores her, but she has no interest in anything more than friendship."

Cole laughed. "Yeah, I know. I tease her all the time about him. Who knows? She could change her mind, but even if she doesn't, he's someone nice for her to go out with. Otherwise, she'd be keeping Deena or one of her other pals company. Not that that's a bad thing, I just think that Mom's got a lot of electricity in that power plant of hers. I'd like to see her have more fun."

"Would you be okay with a step-father?"

Cole laughed. "Yeah, I would, especially Jim. The guy is barely sixty. He ballroom dances, he and his former wife taught dancing, and he's bright and interesting. Obviously he's crazy about Mary McGinnis, so he has good taste."

Jerica laughed. "I can see why anyone would love your mother, she's a sweetheart."

"So," Cole said, "what about a vacation for you? Any plans?"

"No, not this year. I'm too new at the hospital to have a vacation coming. I might go back to Ohio to visit my family for a weekend, but that's it."

"Do you mind living away from them?" he asked.

"A little. I miss all of them, but I never felt like Ohio was home. I suppose that's a strange sentiment, but it's true. I came to Connecticut at eighteen to attend college and I never go back to Ohio except to visit. Even summers, I went home for a week then back to college where I worked for ten weeks each year. After college, I worked in Hartford for two years before taking this job in Mystic."

"It's pretty interesting," Cole began, "that you're back working in the very hospital where you were born."

Jerica smiled. "Yes, it is. And you too, right?"

"Yup, me too."

"I'm looking at the clock on your mantle. It's near eleven. I'm afraid you're not going to find a bookstore open at this time of night."

"Oh well, no problem. I'll watch the news, check out what else is on TV, and hit the hay. I kept you from getting more of your book read too."

"That's ok. It's really been nice to just talk," she said.

"It has," he agreed.

They chatted for a few minutes longer, then reluctantly, they both said goodnight.

Cole sat back in his chair and wished that he was back in his own home with Jerica.

Jerica rested her head against the back of Cole's recliner, petting the cats, wishing he was there.

Chapter Seven

When Cole opened his eyes to the morning sun, he looked at his watch. It was ten past seven. He changed into a pair of jeans and light brown shirt, rolling the sleeves back to just below his elbows.

With a quick comb to his hair he took the key and walked outside. The air felt like it had been washed; the parking lot was damp - it must have rained during the night. He walked a few doors down to the motel's coffee shop where he helped himself to a complimentary apple, doughnut, and cup of black coffee. He took his breakfast outside to a picnic table overlooking a shallow valley in the foreground and blue-gray mountains in the distance. At one point he watched filmy white clouds drift slowly across the granite giants like ghosts slithering away.

When he'd finished his food, he walked back to his room and traded his long sleeved shirt for a gray t-shirt, then he left again and walked about one mile into town. He found a bookstore just opening its doors and went inside when invited by its elderly owner.

"You're an early bird," the white-haired woman said. "Come in, take a look around. Out-of-towner, are you?"

Cole smiled. "Yes, I am."

"Well," she said, "welcome. You go ahead and browse to your heart's content."

"Thanks," he said. Cole found three books he thought he'd enjoy, two fiction novels and one biography about an anthropologist he admired. While there, he also found a beautiful bookmark with a colorful chain full of glass beads attached to it. He bought that for Jerica. In another shop, he purchased some of his mother's coveted little French lavender soaps, a ball for Murphy, and three catnip mice for the cats. He walked back to the motel with his treasures, then set off walking in the opposite direction, away from town. It felt wonderful to be free of schedules and obligations, but when Tuesday morning came in a couple of days, he'd be ready to head for home.

Jerica took care of the cats and Murphy, then she took the dog with her to Mary's. When the older woman greeted Jerica and the excited dog, Mary laughed and gave him a corner of her toast.

"How was last night, Dear? I can't thank you enough. I really enjoyed the evening out."

Jerica smiled. "I'm glad. And I had a very nice night as well. Cole called, by the way, he thought he'd find you there. I explained and we chatted for a bit. He's having a good getaway I think."

"Good," Mary said, "I'm glad he did this. He's usually working around his house or mine. Poor boy, he's so intent on looking after me, and I'm fine."

Jerica smiled as she poured herself a small glass of orange juice. "It's admirable that he's good to you, Mary."

"I know, and I appreciate it. So, what are you up to today? I hope not more work on that computer of yours."

"No, I'm caught up. I should wash my hair, maybe do a little laundry, and then I may read. I borrowed one of Cole's books."

"That sounds pretty relaxing. I'm planning to take things slow too - I'm pooped. Jim had me out on the dance floor half the night. It was fun but tiring. How does a fruit salad sound for lunch? I have some other thoughts for supper, like leftover chicken, but we can figure that out later I guess."

"Fruit salad for lunch sounds good. How about if I pick us up a pizza later? That way, we can be completely lazy, and the best part, no dishes."

Mary laughed at Jerica's suggestion. "I like the way you think, pizza sounds great. After pizza, I'll head over to Cole's for the night."

When the day was through, Jerica went upstairs to shower, change into her pajamas, and finish her book. She thought about the characters, their complicated predicament. She loved the story and she also loved that it was one of Cole's favorites. She wondered: did she love Cole as well?

Just as she climbed into bed and pulled the sheets up to her waist, her cell phone rang. She looked at the display screen and saw that it was Dan.

"Hi," she said.

"Hi, Sweetheart," he began. "Did you miss me? What did you do this weekend?"

Jerica punched her pillow and then lay back against it. "Oh, lots of things, but nothing you'd consider exciting. How was the party?"

"Oh, man, it was wild!" he laughed. "Let me tell you, that's my deal for when you and I get hitched. New York City, here I come!"

Jerica stiffened a bit but said nothing.

"So," he continued, "when do I get to see you? Can you get down here to Hartford?"

"Dan, I can't," she said. "I've got work and it's a long haul for an evening. I think we'll have to wait until next weekend."

"I'll tell you what," he said, "I'll drive to Mystic, let me see, Tuesday night. We'll have dinner. I can't wait to see you."

Tuesday. Cole was coming home on Tuesday. "No, Tuesday won't work," she said.

"Why? What's going on, more meetings or something?"

"Yes," she said, "Tuesday just won't work."

"Let me see, what about Wednesday? I could do Wednesday."

Jerica closed her eyes. Why was she pushing him away? "Okay, Wednesday," she agreed, and when they ended their call, she thought about how relaxing it had been to talk with Cole, and how stressful it had been to talk with Dan. What's happening to me? She wondered. Everything she'd known was less important now. She questioned if her indecision with her career had set this bad mood in motion. She thought about Mary over at Cole's with Murphy and the cats. Lucky Mary. Jerica reached for the light switch, turned off the lamp, then went to sleep.

When Tuesday came, Jerica felt a surge of adrenalin at the thought of Cole coming home. She wasn't sure why, after all, he was simply Mary's son. They had nothing more, except for that one time kiss, and their nearly two hour long telephone conversation while he was in New Hampshire. She pulled her long hair back into a single braid, then slipped into a pale pink dress of soft jersey, a wide black patent leather belt at her waist and black sandals on her feet.

"Jerica, you look adorable," Mary said as she walked into the kitchen with Murphy.

"Thank you," Jerica said. "It's warm today; I thought it would be a good choice."

"It's lovely, Dear. Now, did you remember that Cole will be home later? He called last night while I was at his house. He sounds wonderful and rested. I asked him to dinner but he begged off. Can't blame him. Anyway, he wants us to get together tomorrow night. Are you available?"

Wednesday. Dan. "Oh, Mary, I'm not. I'm so sorry. Dan's coming here from Hartford and we're going out for dinner." Jerica felt truly saddened, she so longed to see Cole.

Mary's face reflected her disappointment. "Well, these things happen. We'll have other times, Dear."

Jerica went to work and thought often of Cole. Where was he at nine? Where was he at noon? Where was he at three? When she turned into Mary's driveway at six, Cole's car was there. Jerica's heart felt like it was going to vibrate out of her chest. She straightened her hair a bit then walked as casually as she could into Mary's kitchen. He was there, sitting with his mother, drinking a glass of black iced coffee. He appraised her from head to toes, deciding that the pink dress made her look like a nicely packaged treat of cotton candy.

"Hi," she said.

"Hi yourself," he returned.

"I see you made it home safely," she said and then regretted the nonsensical words.

"Yes, I did."

He wasn't making this easy.

"Jerica," Mary began, "sit down with us. What can I get you to drink?"

"Nothing, thank you, Mary. I'm fine." Jerica sat down wondering what, if anything, she had to say.

"Cole's been telling me all about Boston and New Hampshire," his mother said.

Cole's eyes met Jerica's. After a few moments he stood and reached for a small bag which he placed before Jerica. "A little something for you," he said.

She opened the bag to find the beautiful bookmark. Her eyes glistened and she nearly cried, but she managed not to be too obviously touched as she thanked him for such a wonderful thoughtful gift.

"And he brought me lavender soaps, my favorites," Mary said.

Jerica smiled at Mary and Cole. "You've raised a thoughtful son," she said.

"I wish I could convince him to stay for dinner," Mary said.

"Not tonight, Mom. I want to get home to Murphy and the whiskers. It was a fun trip, but there really is no place like home."

"I know," Mary said. "I'm giving you a hard time, but I really understand."

"I think I'll get going," he said as he finished his coffee and stood. "Nice to see you, Jerica," he said and then he leaned forward to hug his mother. "Thanks, Mom. I'll talk to you later."

Mary walked outside with Cole and Jerica backed away, turning to walk up to her own rooms. Once there, she spotted Cole's book and ran downstairs with it in her hands. She went outside and met Mary coming in.

"I have Cole's book," she said as she raced past Mary and reached his car as he was about to back into the street.

"Cole!" she called to him.

He stopped with his foot on the brake and then he put the car into park.

"Here's your book. Thank you for allowing me to borrow it. I loved it."

Cole accepted the worn volume from her and smiled, saying nothing. She tucked a few strands of hair back toward the loosened braid and he watched.

"What?" she asked, "I'm a mess, right?"

He nearly said absolutely not, but instead he said, "Come on home with me."

Jerica felt stunned. "What?"

"Get in my car and come home with me," he said easily.

"Why?"

Cole smiled. "I thought you might like to trade this book in for the other, Come Spring."

"Oh, yes I would, but I'll get it another time. Thanks anyway." She knew her voice had to sound shaky, because she definitely felt that way, and she definitely would have loved to go shamefully home with him.

"I heard you have plans for tomorrow night and can't join us," he said.

"That's true," she said softly, "but it will give you and your mother some nice time together. Maybe the three of us could have another night for a cookout or something. Summer's about over; I can't believe there's just a few days before I see those big yellow buses on the road again."

Cole lowered his head then looked up at her pretty face. "Yup, and me in front of a blackboard. The summer flew by as it always does."

"We can still cook out, right? I'll make things for it, and I know your mom will too."

"Sure," Cole said, "we've got lots of time before the first snow flies. We'll plan one for later in the week."

"Okay," she said, "I'll think about what to make, and I'll mention it to your mother."

"Good. We'll do it," he said, his eyes fastened on hers.

"Okay then," she said, yet neither of them moved for several seconds.

"I should go," he said, "Murphy will be crossing his legs."

Jerica laughed. "He'll be happy to see you."

"Sure you don't want to come along?" he asked as he shifted into reverse, his foot on the brake and a smile on his face.

"Go," she said softly, "they're waiting for you."

Without further words, Cole moved out of the driveway and headed for home. Jerica stood and watched until his car turned a corner and was out of sight. She wasn't sure why, but she missed him still, as if he were hundreds of miles away.

Chapter Eight

In late September, Jerica told Mary that she was taking that Friday off from work and was flying to Ohio for the weekend to see her family. She didn't mention the trip to Cole; she wasn't sure he'd care. There were times when he was intense with her, to the point where she'd have loved leaning in to his arms. But there were other times when he seemed cool, keeping an emotional and physical distance. She didn't know what to make of it, and she didn't know what was going on with her *own* feelings.

Dan had coerced her into weekends in Hartford and other times to his parents' home in Stamford. Although they had all been welcoming and kind to her, Jerica felt displaced. They dined at a hand-carved mahogany table large enough to accommodate at least twenty people. The fireplace mantles were made of imported Italian marble and the light fixtures were custom made with hand-blown glass. It was a different world, with a maid, a cook, and a gardener. Jerica thought about the difference between the life style at Dan's and the average life she'd grown up with. Her comfort zone more coincided with that of Mary and Cole McGinnis. She liked the creative freedom offered with warm blends of inherited and mismatched furnishings. All of the Walters' possessions were well put together by an interior designer. There were no indications of preference for color or collections. This would not be the way in which she would live should she end up with Dan.

"When you leave for Ohio," Mary said, "I'd like you to take something to your parents for me. I have the cutest picture of Cole peeking into your carriage. You can just see your sweet little face, those attentive eyes looking back at Cole. And in the background, there's your old house. I think your folks will love it. I'm picking up a frame for it today, so it will be ready for you to take along."

"They'll treasure it, Mary, and I'll be anxious to see it too. I'm happy to be making this trip. I miss them and my sister's baby girl has probably changed so much since I was last there. I know I want to stay here in the east, and preferably in Mystic, but I need to make certain that I get back to Ohio more often."

"I know what you mean," Mary said. "Time has a way of slipping past."

On Friday, Jerica chose to wear tan slacks with a white blouse and a navy blue blazer. She packed a small bag, the framed picture from Mary inside among her clothes, and she was gone.

Mary couldn't believe how much she missed this sweet girl. After Cole, she would have liked another child, but it wasn't to be. She would have adored a little girl just like Jerica.

When she arrived back at Mary's late Sunday night, Jerica found Mary waiting up for her in the living room.

"Mary, I hope I didn't cause you to stay up until nearly midnight. My plane was delayed; it can be so tiring to fly these days."

"Don't worry about me at all, Dear. I'm happy to see you. How did it go? Is your family well?"

Jerica sat down on the sofa across from Mary. "They're all doing fine. My parents are in good health, my brother's doing great at college, and my sister and I actually had a night out together. Her baby is big and beautiful now. It was nice. I'm so glad I went, but I'm glad to be home."

Home. It had just slipped out, but the feelings were accurate. This place, the town, the people, it felt like home.

Mary smiled. The word home had not gone unnoticed by her. "You must be tired," she said. "We can talk more later. You go ahead upstairs and get settled in."

"Thank you," Jerica said as she stood. "And Mary, they loved the picture you sent; it went right up on top of the mantle. I have a box of

Mom and Dad's favorite candy they sent to you and Cole. I'll sort out my travel bag and give it to you in the morning."

"They needn't have sent a thing, but it was so good of them to think of Cole and me. Go and rest, Dear, you must be exhausted."

Jerica wanted to ask about Cole, but if there had been anything negative or important, Mary would have told her. She went upstairs, showered quickly, then went to bed.

In the morning, Jerica brushed her long hair and selected a basic forest green dress and matching shoes to wear to work. Before she left her room upstairs, she took the box of candy from her travel bag and placed it down on the kitchen table. When Mary saw the package, neatly tied with a blue satin ribbon, she smiled.

"This will be very much enjoyed," she said. "Thank you, Dear."

"You're welcome," Jerica replied as the two embraced lightly. "I'm off to work. I'll grab tea and a muffin there later. And I'll see you this evening."

When evening came, Dan arrived to take Jerica out for dinner. Mary had changed into a lightweight pants suit to go out with her son and she hoped that before Cole arrived, Jerica and Dan would have gone off. Her wish came true - they left about five minutes before Cole showed up in her kitchen.

"Ready for our big date, Mom?" Cole teased. "I hope Jim doesn't see us out on the town."

"Now stop that, Cole McGinnis," she said. "Let's go, I'm ready to eat the hind end off of something."

Cole smiled and drove his mother to a dockside restaurant they both favored. They were seated by a window overlooking the quaint harbor and selected a white wine to go with their meals.

As they talked and watched the harbor activity, Mary caught sight of Jerica and Dan sitting at a corner table. She had never seen them out together and she felt slightly stunned. When he noticed his mother's mood, Cole turned and followed her gaze. His eyes went directly to Jerica who did not notice Cole and Mary at all. Cole turned around and looked at his mother, his eyebrows raised slightly. "Guess this was a popular choice," he said.

"Would you prefer to go someplace else?" Mary asked. "We could get our food packed up and have it at home."

Cole shook his head. "No, we'll stay right here in this perfect spot and we'll eat our dinner. It's okay, Mom, really."

Mary scowled. "Alright," she said, "we'll talk about something else. So, how's everything at school?"

"Good, on a two-fold measure."

"What do you mean?" Mary asked.

"I'm settled in at the high school, I have a good class this year, and I've registered for two new college courses which I'll attend two evenings starting next week."

"That's wonderful," Mary said. "Is this to prepare for teaching college?"

"Probably. I'm thinking that way, but it'll take another year, so I'll have time to figure things out."

"I'm so proud of you, Honey. This is great news."

Cole outlined the courses he planned to take. He was enthused and she liked that his mind was on something positive.

"Do you have any particular school in mind where you'd like to teach?" Mary asked.

"Someplace local: no doubt about that. I'll hang in teaching at the high school level until I get something nearby. I wouldn't mind Wingate; it's a good school, even though it's a community college. That would probably be my first choice."

Mary listened proudly, sipped her wine, and turned with Cole to watch the harbor boats coming and going. Cole stole a look toward Jerica. She looked beautiful as she gave her attention to Dan who was animated in his gestures, telling her about something. Cole still would have enjoyed socking the guy.

With after dinner coffee, Mary decided to inquire about Kathy. She wanted the girl in Cole's life to love him and only him, and, as much as she favored Jerica, Mary was fearful that a relationship there could prove to be a heartbreaker for her son.

"So, have you been in contact with that Kathy Bezanson?" she asked.

"Yeah, but not often. She's a nice girl, but Atlanta's a hike for a date," he said with a smile.

"I guess so," Mary agreed. "So, do you two talk on the phone? E-mail?"

"The phone," Cole said. "E-mail has its purposes, but it's not very satisfactory for a social relationship. I like to hear the tone of a person's voice. I called her to check on her flight back to Georgia. After that, we started ping-ponging the calls."

"So," Mary said, trying not to pry, "you talk to her once in a while."

"Yup, maybe once a week. I called her last Sunday evening. There's no intensity to what we have. She's interesting and attractive. If she weren't so darn far away, I'd probably see her now and then."

"What about Jerica?" Mary asked softly.

"I don't know, what about her? It looks like she's all set with her friend Dan."

"That doesn't change your feelings."

Cole looked out to the harbor, then back to his mother. "It's all right, Mom. You worry too much. I have no expectations about Jerica. Sure, she's great, but she's not available."

Mary shook her head. "I'm very fond of that girl. Oh, her folks sent a beautiful box of candy for you and me. I'd like you to take it home with you, or else I'll eat it! I'll drop them a line to thank them, but you might mention it to Jerica when you see her again."

"Sure," he said and they both turned again to watch the now sleepy harbor and the brilliant sunset settle across the horizon.

"Would you like to go?" Mary asked.

"That depends," Cole said. "How about a little stroll on the docks? The air is beautiful out there. You can actually smell autumn on its way. Are you game?"

"I'd love it," Mary said, and they left the restaurant, now noticed by Jerica. She watched the two walk out the door and around toward the water, her eyes riveted to their movement.

"What're you looking at?" Dan asked.

Jerica struggled to turn her attention back to her companion. "Oh, it's Mary McGinnis and her son. They just left the restaurant; I didn't realize they were in here."

Dan grimaced. "Who cares?" He reached across the table to take her hands in his. Jerica smiled slightly and forced herself to concentrate on Dan. He'd driven a long way to be with her, and it was the least she could do.

"What's next for us?" he asked.

Jerica looked surprised. "What do you mean?"

"Us," he said. "When are we shopping for a diamond? I'd like for us to make plans, Sweetheart, it's been long enough."

"I don't know," she said. "I feel in transition. I'm not sure how long I'll stay with this job. I love the hospital, but not in administration."

"But," Dan said, "that has nothing to do with us. If you dislike the job, quit. Come back and live in Hartford."

"I need a job," Jerica said, thinking that she didn't want city life, she wanted Mystic.

"You don't need a job as my wife," Dan said. "We could buy a house, get started on our lives."

Jerica looked out through the window but could no longer see Mary or Cole. She wondered if they'd gone home.

"Tell me you'll think about it, Sweetheart. You know how I love you. I think you need to get out of this one-horse town and back to Hartford. Maybe someday we could even live in New York City. What a place! I love it there."

"I like New York too, Dan, but living there isn't in my plans or hopes. I like a country atmosphere."

"Well," he said, "let's put that conversation on the back burner. All I can think of now is us, getting us together. Think about it."

Jerica decided to be as agreeable as possible. Dan meant well, but sometimes it seemed their thoughts traveled in different directions.

"I'll think about it, Dan, I promise."

Chapter Nine

It was a few days later before Jerica saw Cole again. When she did, it was at his mother's while he replaced broken bricks in her front pathway. Watching him work from her window upstairs, Jerica wanted to go down to where he was. She didn't know what she'd say, but it didn't matter. She simply wanted to be near to him, to breathe the same air. After several minutes, she pushed herself away from the window and lay on her back across the bed. Saturday. She stared at the white ceiling. There should be something fun in this day, but she also had laundry to do and her rooms could use a vacuuming and dusting. She decided to go downstairs for a cup of tea, then she'd get started. At least in the evening she had plans with Dan, maybe she'd even surprise him by offering to go into Hartford for a night on the town.

In the kitchen, Jerica heated a cup of water in the microwave and then added a tea bag. As the tea steeped, she looked out to Mary's backyard. The leaves were beginning to change colors, many to their brilliant orange-red; New England was the place to be in autumn.

"Hi," Cole said as he walked into the kitchen from the front hallway.

"Hi," Jerica replied with an air of surprise in her voice.

"Any idea where Mom is?" he asked.

"Yes, she ran over to Deena's for a while. She said she'd be home by noon."

"Oh, okay. I replaced and reset a few bricks out front. Frost heaves broke a couple; I thought they might trip someone up, best to get them in order before the cold sets in again. So, how're you doing? Anything exciting going on?"

"No, not really. I made myself some tea, want some?"

"No, thanks. Maybe I'll grab a bottle of water though." He moved to the refrigerator and then sat down at the kitchen table. Jerica had planned to take her tea upstairs, but now she joined him in one of Mary's comfortable old oak chairs.

They looked at one another. When the awkward moment passed, Cole said, "What's happening this weekend? Big plans?"

"Nothing in particular, we may do an evening in Hartford, I'm not sure. What about you?"

Cole drank from his water bottle then replied, "Well, the rest of today will be spent working on the house. I'm anxious to get it done, I've been living in limbo and I'd like to finish it up. Tomorrow I'll correct papers, maybe take a walk with Murphy, other than that, I don't know."

"What about night life?" Jerica asked. "Don't you like to get out and do something different? Go to a club or something?"

He looked at her for several seconds then said, "Sometimes, but I wouldn't have taken you for a club type. Is that what you like to do?"

Jerica laughed. "No, I'm not really the club type. I like to go out dancing once in a while, hear some music, but I'm happy with pizza and a movie, or even a good book and a pot of tea."

Cole nodded. They were silent for a few minutes and then he asked, "Are you thinking of going to Ohio for Thanksgiving?"

Jerica looked perplexed. She hadn't thought that far ahead; they were just into the beginnings of October. "I don't know," she said. My parents and brother may go to my sister's house again this year. I went last year and it was quite the crowd. She had seven of her in-laws, six from our family, and a few neighbors." Jerica smiled at Cole. "It was fun, but I hardly had a chance to visit with anyone. I might just stay here this year."

"Wouldn't you go to your boyfriend's family?"

Jerica's heart lurched. It felt uncomfortable to talk about Dan as her boyfriend to Cole. "I don't think so," she said. She didn't explain and he didn't ask her to. When she'd been to the Walters' for dinners, it had been very elaborate, not the warmth she longed for.

"Well," he began, "if you're around, you're welcome to join my mother and me. Sometimes we pick up my aunt, but there are times when she goes to one of her four kids, so we'll see."

"So there could be just you and your Mom?"

"Yup. We used to do these huge dinners with about a dozen of us. But now that my grandparents are gone, and my cousins are all grown, moved, or married, things have changed. The past few years, Mom and I make dinner together here. We take a walk if the weather permits, and when we're literally stuffed, we watch White Christmas."

Jerica smiled. "I love that movie. Your Thanksgiving sounds wonderful."

Cole stood and tossed his water bottle into the recycling container. "Well, I'm hitting the road. And the invitation stands. If you're here in Mystic, we'll put you to work peeling potatoes or something."

"Thanks," she replied, and when he left, she stood and watched until she could no longer see him. Jerica hugged her arms across her chest. Everything about him warms my heart.

Jerica thought about the coming holidays - she loved them. She already knew that she'd be going to Ohio for Christmas, but Thanksgiving was an uncertainty.

When Mary came back from Deena's, she found Jerica peeling and slicing apples at the kitchen sink.

"Oh," she said with a smile, "this looks interesting. What are you making?"

Jerica didn't stop working for more than a moment but she returned the smile and said, "I bought these great apples yesterday on my way home from work. I forgot about them being in my car overnight, but after Cole left, I remembered and decided to use some of them to make an apple cake. I hope that's ok."

"Of course it is," Mary replied, "and the house is going to smell fabulous."

Jerica smiled. "It will. I love the aroma of cinnamon and nutmeg baking in something. My mother used to make gingerbread and you could smell it from outside the house. How's your friend, Deena?"

Mary sat down after pouring herself a cup of coffee. "She's doing pretty well. The swelling is going down; it looks like the surgery was a good move. She's still nervous about navigating the grocery store on her own, so I took her to pick up a few things. I think it did her good to get out. So, I missed my boy?"

"Yes," Jerica said as she sliced the last of eight apples. "He replaced a few of your bricks in the front walk."

"Oh," Mary said, "that's Cole. I'm glad he did that, but he amazes me. I think he stores these tasks in his mind; he never lets things get out of hand. I'm very fortunate to have a son like Cole. I have friends who aren't so lucky."

Jerica washed her hands and then sat down across from Mary. "You two have an enviable relationship," she said.

Mary looked at the beautiful young woman and placed her coffee cup back on its saucer. "I know. How about you? Are you and your parents close?"

"Yes, Mom and I are very similar. We always loved baking together or doing some kind of craft project. I was two when my sister came along and nearly four when my brother was born. We all got along great, but when they got a bit older, I think it was evident that Mom and I liked to do creative things and they didn't. By the time I was twelve or thirteen, I could feel Mom being restrained, almost like she didn't want to show favoritism by doing so many things with me." Jerica smiled. "Then I got to thinking the same way, so some of that fun stuff stopped."

"That's too bad," Mary said as she thought that Jerica's expression revealed a sense of sadness.

"It was okay, I understood," Jerica said. "My sister and brother were such sweet children, and I wouldn't have wanted them to feel left out. Not that Mom and I left them out - it's just that they weren't into the baking and creative things."

"What about now? Are your mother and sister close?"

"Yes, and with the baby in the picture, that's brought them especially close. My sister married while in college, and she's a young mother." Jerica laughed, "My mom is the classic grandmother: that little girl is going to get plenty of loving attention."

Mary smiled and sipped her coffee.

"I think I'll go ahead and make the cake if that's ok. I'm seeing Dan tonight so while this is baking, I thought I'd do a few things like dust and vacuum upstairs. Is there anything I can do for you, Mary?"

"Not a thing, thank you, Dear. I vacuumed and dusted down here yesterday, so maybe I'll work on getting my gardens ready for the cold. Some things need cutting back, and some of my bulbs need to come into the cellar before we get a freeze. Goodness, I can't believe the holidays are so near. It sneaks up on me."

Jerica measured sugar and flour into a bowl. "Cole was talking about Thanksgiving," she said. "He invited me to join you if I don't go to Ohio."

"Oh," Mary said. "I'm glad he did that. We're a small family now, but we manage to have a wonderful time. There's nothing like taking a walk in the chilled air and then coming into a house filled with those festive aromas. I love every tiny particle of the coming season. I'm afraid I turn into a four-year old."

Jerica laughed. "Good, you'll be easy to Christmas shop for; I'll just buy you a toy!"

Mary laughed. "Go right ahead; I'd love it."

The cake was made and placed in the oven with the timer set for thirty minutes. Jerica scurried about starting a small batch of laundry, then tidying up her rooms. After that, she decided to check her wardrobe for the dress she would wear out with Dan. He favored her in red. She selected a deep blue dress she would wear with a wide brown belt at her waist.

When she returned to the kitchen to check on the status of the cake, Mary was there, about to lift it from the oven. "The timer went off, Dear. I'll let you take over."

"Okay," Jerica agreed, "I'll set it up on the stove top to cool gradually if it won't be in your way."

"Nope, that's fine," Mary said. "It smells so good. Will you take that to your Dan?"

"Oh, no," Jerica was quick to reply. "He's not a sweet eater. He'd eat the apple plain, and I'll take him a few, but no, he won't eat cake or pie or anything that isn't nutritionally sound."

Mary didn't think Dan sounded like any fun at all.

Chapter Ten

Early Saturday evening, Jerica drove to Hartford and met Dan for a night out with a few friends. At eleven, she said she was tired and thought she'd head home.

"Stay the night," Dan begged. "You shouldn't be driving alone this time of night; it's a long haul."

"I've done it before," she said, "I'll be fine."

"Why not stay?" Dan asked, rubbing her knee slowly. "We could have a nice breakfast together and a walk in the park. Come on, stay."

Jerica rubbed her eyes. "Not tonight," she said. "I'd like to go back. I have things to do tomorrow, odds and ends."

Dan frowned, "I can't wait until we're married; I don't like this." Jerica gave him a half smile. She was leaving.

Sunday brought sunshine and Jerica was feeling tired but glad to be home. She stretched, pulled the covers up to her chin, and then thought about what she might do for the day. Out of bed and shuffling about, she slipped into a warm, burgundy robe and slippers then went downstairs, following the aroma of coffee.

"Good morning, Dear," Mary greeted her from behind the Sunday paper. "There's fresh coffee, and whatever you'd like for breakfast. Eggs, toast, fruit, cereal - help yourself to whatever appeals to you."

"I think I'll have coffee and a piece of apple cake. It's Sunday, I don't have to be practical today."

Mary smiled. "You're right. Cut me a piece too."

Jerica laughed. "Partners in crime," she said cutting into the moist cake. "I'm surprised you didn't have some of this before now."

"Oh, I wasn't around long after you left yesterday. Jim called and asked me to see a movie with him. I got in around eleven, watched the news, and went up to bed. How was your night in Hartford?"

Jerica shrugged her shoulders softly. "It was okay. Dan has these friends he works with - we met up with them for a while."

Mary nibbled on her cake and nodded.

"What do you have planned for today?" Jerica asked between sips of coffee.

"Nothing earth shattering," Mary said. "What about you?"

Jerica looked out through the window to the beautiful fall day. "I'm thinking I might explore a bit of Mystic. I haven't been to the museum yet, and I really haven't taken the time to browse the shops."

Mary looked at the young woman, so lovely, yet lonely. "Are there any girls your age at the hospital?"

"Oh, yes, but I haven't really gotten to know them, they're mostly the nursing staff. In admin, I'm the youngest." Jerica said.

Mary nodded. "Well, I'm planning dinner for four o'clock. I hope you'll join Cole and me; there's always plenty."

The thought of an opportunity to see Cole was more than interesting, and Mary was a wonderful cook. "Thank you," Jerica said. "What can I contribute to the feast?"

Mary laughed. "I don't know about the feast part, it's a simple meal, but don't worry about a thing, Dear, enjoy your Mystic adventure and then come home for dinner."

"Okay," Jerica said, "I'll plan on being back by three or three-thirty at the latest."

In jeans, a tan jersey, and a light-weight red jacket, Jerica drove to the waterfront and parked her car. She went first to the museum near the docks, then out to walk around a couple of historic vessels. The weather couldn't have been better, cool and clear, and among the other tourists, she fit in perfectly.

In one of the shops she found a tiny hooded sweatshirt, the name Mystic on its front, that she thought would fit her little niece. She purchased that and a dozen lemon squares to add to Mary's dinner menu. Jerica felt like a high school girl with a crush. She couldn't wait to see Cole.

"Hey, can I give you a lift, little girl?" she heard a familiar male voice ask. She turned and saw Cole in his car, leaning over to the passenger's side to speak to her. It was a surprise to see him. She'd been thinking of him and hoped her expression hadn't given that away.

"Hi," she said. "I have my car nearby, but thanks. What are you doing here?"

"I need another box of finish nails; this hardware store is where I pick up most of my supplies."

"Oh. Well, I guess I'll see you later at your mother's for dinner?"

"Wouldn't miss it," Cole said, and then he was gone. She watched him pull away and then she walked on, stopping for a cup of hot cider. Jerica found an unoccupied bench and sat down. The water was a deep blue, sketched with white streaks from wind dancing and disturbing the sea's surface. She wondered why anyone would want to live anywhere else.

At three, Jerica pulled into Mary's driveway and saw Cole's car. She took the two packages, the gift for her sister's baby and the lemon squares, and walked around to the back of the house to the kitchen door. She found Cole outside tossing a Frisbee to Murphy. When the dog spotted her, he abandoned the game and ran to her. Jerica laughed as Cole stood, one hand on his hip, his dark brown eyes following Murphy's prance toward this very pretty young woman.

"I guess I know who matters to him!" Cole said.

Jerica patted Murphy's head and told him how handsome he was.

"Maybe he just likes lemon squares," she said as she held up the white bakery box.

Cole held the screen door open as Jerica and Murphy walked into Mary's aromatic kitchen.

Dinner and dessert were dotted with conversation about Cole's classes to complete his Master's program and his plans to eventually obtain a doctorate in education.

"You've set high goals for yourself. Are you excited about the possibility of teaching at the college level?" Jerica asked.

Cole pursed his lips and sat back in his chair, his left forefinger looped through the handle of his coffee cup. "Yeah, I am. When I

73

started college more than ten years ago, I had those thoughts of studying to become an architect. Then I began to realize that meant travel to some extent and I didn't want that. After a couple of other career ideas, teaching won."

Jerica sipped her coffee and thought about how wonderful it must feel to be in a career you so loved. She'd made a mistake going into the business end of things. She wished fervently that she could do something else, something meaningful.

The following Thursday evening, around eight, the phone rang.

"Jerica?" Cole's voice had an air of surprise in it when she said hello.

"Yes, hi, Cole."

"Hi. Is Mom around? Everything all right over there?"

"Everything's fine. Your mother is enjoying a warm soak."

"Okay," he said, "I suppose that's a good indication that she won't want to get dressed and come out on a cold night."

Jerica laughed. "Probably not. Did you need her for something?"

"It's these crazy curtains I bought for the dining room. The room's finished except for putting up these darn things. I can't get them right, and I was hoping to persuade Mom to help me."

Jerica smiled, envisioning the struggle between man and material.

"Would you like me to run over and help? I can probably figure them out. I don't have your mother's experience, but at least I'm a woman."

"What's that supposed to mean?" he asked.

Jerica laughed. "Take it or leave it: do you want me to assist you?"

There was a hesitation on his part and then he replied, "Okay, if you don't mind."

"I don't mind," she said. "I'll tell your mother I'm leaving and I'll be over in about ten minutes."

When he opened the door to her, she covered her mouth and laughed. He had one blue and white curtain over his left shoulder, another draped over his right arm. He looked like he was going to a toga party.

After she helped him to hang the swags with full-length straight side panels, they stood back to appreciate the attractive affect. "Can I get you something to drink?" he asked.

"Do you have cider by any chance?"

"No, I usually have it this time of year, I'm sorry. I have soda, OJ, coffee, tea, or water."

"I'll have water," she said as she sat down in his kitchen rocking chair. He sat across from her, a cup of coffee in his hands.

"I wouldn't have gotten those things up without you," he said. "Thanks for coming over."

"No problem," she said. "I like that room - all the blues work so well together, and I like the simplicity of the mantle with just the sailboat and a few shells. That's your only nautical room, isn't it?"

"Yup. I had some old blue and white plates from my grandparents' things. I decided that to do them justice, the dining room should be blue. The ocean's blue, so it kind of fell into place to do a nautical theme. But, a decorator I'm not."

"It doesn't matter," Jerica said. "It all looks so inviting; I love your house."

To that statement, Cole had no response. He looked at her for a moment then reached down to pat Murphy who lay at his feet.

"I should go," Jerica said as she stood and left her water bottle at the sink. "It's after ten, and we both have work in the morning."

"True," Cole said as he stood. "Come on. Murph and I will see you to your car. Thanks again, Jerica, I appreciate you helping me out."

"Anytime," she said.

When they reached her car, she unlocked the door and he opened it for her. She slid behind the wheel, looked up at Cole, and then started the engine. It all felt so normal, so completely relaxing to be in his presence. Cole McGinnis had seemed from the beginning to be part of her, like her eyes, her arms, her breathing. She put her foot on the brake then shifted the car into reverse and drove away.

For Cole, having her there and now gone, left him feeling like something important was missing. He wondered if she'd always held a place in his being, subconsciously or consciously, from the time of her birth. He wasn't sure he believed in destiny, but whatever this magnetic feeling was, he understood that she impacted his life.

75

Cole walked back inside with Murphy, tempted to once again lay his hand on the arm of the rocking chair where she had been sitting, but he resisted. "I've got to stop this," he murmured softly as the dog looked up at him. "She's not ours, Murph," he said, and then he started turning off lights in preparation for the close of the day.

Chapter Eleven

On November first, Cole was driving to his teaching position at the high school when he thought about Jerica. He'd been busy with graduate school two nights a week, which prohibited him from stopping by his mother's as often as he'd like. Between correcting homework for the high school kids and completing his own assignments, plus taking care of a house and pets, he wondered where his free time went. His home was pretty much completed, just two of the four bedrooms still wore the old wallpaper; he wasn't in a hurry to tackle them, they were fine for now. *Maybe,* he thought, *it's time for a dinner to officially celebrate the house.* He'd invite his mother, and if she approved, Jim, and then, of course, there was Jerica.

"Hi Mom," he began his phone call that evening. "How's everything going?"

"Good, Honey. How about with you?"

"Busy, but otherwise, no complaints. I feel like going back to school was a definite move in the right direction."

"That's wonderful," Mary said. "I know it takes a lot of effort, but it'll be worth it in the end."

"Yeah, that's what I think too. And, I've been thinking of throwing my house a renewal party, a little dinner to take pleasure in more than three years of getting the place shipshape. What do you think?"

"I think the idea is a brilliant one. Just tell me when and I'll be happy to cook up a storm."

Cole smiled. "That sounds good, and I'll put some things together, maybe I'll do steaks on the grill."

"In November?" she asked.

"Sure, why not? The grill works fine in the cold."

"Oh, that's a great idea. Who will you invite?"

Cole rubbed his eyes then sat down. "I thought we might invite Jim, if you're willing, and Jerica. I'd ask a few people I work with, but it might seem like I'm showing off. I am, but what the heck!"

Mary laughed. "Well, a small dinner party would be perfectly okay. As for Jim, I see no reason not to invite him. He's kind of like a barnacle, if you know what I mean, but I enjoy his company. I'm sure he'd love to come, he's mentioned your house to me a few times."

"Right, that's the deal then. We'll do it. How about next Sunday around four? It will be getting dark. I can have a fire going in a couple of the fireplaces, really set the mood."

"And," Mary began, "for whom is this mood being set?"

Cole was glad that his mother couldn't read the expression he knew to be on his face. "Just the mood in general," he said.

"Uh-huh," Mary McGinnis replied. "Well, shall I invite Jim or would you like to give him a call?"

"I'll call him," Cole said, "and I'll call Jerica too."

When Cole placed the phone back on its receiver, he sat for a few moments, his eyes closed.

The following evening, after speaking briefly with Cole about his invitation, Jerica sat down on her bed and then rolled over onto her side in a fetal position. At last, she thought, I'll see him. It felt like it had been months, when actually it had only been two weeks. She thought about what she would offer to make to contribute to the dinner, and she thought about a gift, a token to congratulate him on a home to be proud of.

She thought about Dan too. He'd been completely charming when she'd met him at college, and he continued trying hard to be the person to win Jerica's affections. She wasn't sure why she'd always felt flattered yet hesitant about him; she wondered if it was an immaturity level, a man not fully developed. It was so different with Cole. At just past twenty-nine he had so much of his life together. He made her feel safe, like he knew what he was doing all the time; this was a man in whom she could trust.

On Sunday at four, they gathered together. Cole cooked steaks on the grill as planned and tossed a salad. Mary made her famous scalloped potato dish and butternut squash, and Jerica made a four-layer spice cake with creamed cheese frosting. Jim provided a bottle of wine. The dinner, served in Cole's blue dining room, was delicious and festive. The hearth was inviting with a snapping, steady glow provided by aromatic fruitwood logs. Amidst the simple sailing vessel and shells on his mantle, Cole had placed a few clear glass votives with white candles, and they too added warmth to the assembly.

"This is remarkable, Cole," Jim said as he looked around. "I'm amazed at what you've accomplished in this old house. It's wonderful, and thank you for including me in this evening."

"I agree with Jim," Mary said. "You're my son and it may not be polite to brag, but Honey, this house is now a beautiful home."

Cole smiled and thanked them. Jerica looked at each dear face; she didn't know what she could add, but felt it was her turn to say something.

"It makes me very envious," she said, "It's the kind of home anyone would appreciate. I love coming here."

Cole looked at her seated directly across the table from him. Her beautiful face reflected a pure truth and sweet spirit. "Thank you," he said, "and thank you all for coming here tonight to fill this old place with joy. I hope you'll come here often."

Their wine glasses met for a tinkling touch: a promise to the future.

"Jim and I collaborated on something for you," Mary said, "something to add even more joy!"

Jim laughed and said, "Let me get it, Mary. You sit and sip that wine."

Mary winked at Cole and Jerica as Jim moved a large package from one of the dining room chairs and delivered it to Cole.

"Well, this is great," he said, "early Christmas." Cole untied the package to find a nice wooden wine rack and twelve assorted bottles of red and white wines. "Wow," he said, "this is terrific; you'll have to come back and help me drink this. Thank you."

Jerica stood and walked to where she'd left her purse. She placed a large object, draped with a pretty dishtowel, on his lap.

"I saw this at a shop near the docks," she said, "I thought it would sit nicely on your dining room hearth."

Cole pulled the cloth from a beautiful, contorted piece of driftwood, upon which Jerica had fastened a large blue bow. Cole's eyes met hers as she moved back to her chair across from him.

"This is perfect," he said, "thank you." Her eyes told him he was welcome.

Mary and Jim looked at one another and smiled.

"That's a wonderfully thoughtful gift, Jerica," Mary said. "And that cake you made is heavenly. This has been a memorable evening."

"I'm thrilled to have been included," Jim said.

"I'm glad you could join us, Jim," Cole began. "It was a long time coming, but worth every minute of sanding and nailing."

Mary looked at each one of them, together they formed a warm team. "We should go," she said. "Jim has an early day tomorrow - a seminar in Providence at eight."

"That's an early start for you," Cole said. "It will take you an hour or so to get there."

"Yes," Jim agreed, "but I'm an early riser, so it's not too bad."

Mary stood and carried dishes to the kitchen along with Jerica. The two men followed their example and helped to clear the table.

"Do you want some help with these, Honey?" Mary asked.

"Not at all. I've got it covered. Jerica's helping with the clean up, right?" he said with a smile toward her.

She laughed and gave Murphy a pat on the head. "Yes," she said, "I'll help you."

"You two," Jim said, "are quite the pair, like a brother and sister."

Cole and Jerica looked at one another, both of them thinking the same thing; they certainly didn't feel a brother-sister connection.

"Okay," Mary said with a smile on her pretty face, "we'll go along and leave you two young ones to the clean up. See? There are some advantages to growing older."

"And," Jim added, "the alternative to growing older isn't particularly appealing!"

Everyone laughed and then Mary and Jim left.

"Well, thanks for the invitation to help with the dishes," Jerica teased. "Let's get started."

Cole smiled as he placed the wine rack in a corner of his kitchen. "I was just kidding," he said. "Come and sit down. I'll do this kitchen stuff later. And by the way, I have cider."

Jerica smiled. "Good, I'll have some in the rocker after clean up. I'm a woman of my word; we're doing dishes first."

"Right, Boss," he said. "Wash or dry?"

"I'll wash," she said as she rolled her sleeves back.

He watched her, every part of her intriguing, enchanting. He wondered how he would get over her. And then he reminded himself to live in the moment. She was here, now, and later could be dealt with when it must.

With leftovers wrapped and put away, and dishes done, Cole offered Jerica that promised cider.

"Warm or cold?" he asked.

"Warm please, with a touch of cinnamon."

"Will cinnamon sticks do?" he asked.

Jerica sat down in the rocker she'd claimed as her own. "You thought of everything, didn't you? Yes, the cinnamon sticks would be delightful, thank you."

Cole heated cider in the microwave then stirred each one, leaving the cinnamon sticks in the cups. He placed one on the kitchen table before Jerica, the other he held and sat down across from her.

"We always end up in my kitchen," he said.

Jerica sipped the warm drink and smiled. "I think most people enjoy hovering around in the kitchen, but of course, your kitchen is especially inviting. It's big and square, cozy, and this rocking chair is so perfect here. This is definitely my favorite room."

"Well then," Cole stood, "if we're staying here, we should at least have some music." He turned the dial on the counter radio until he found some contemporary tunes. They both listened, content to be in one another's company, and then they both laughed as an oldie came along, a twist. Jerica stood, placed her cider down on the table, and motioned for Cole to join her for a dance.

"I don't think so," he said, and then she reached for his hand and pulled him up to her. She laughed watching him go all the way down, like a pro, really getting into his groove. When the twist ended, a slow piece came on and for a moment, they looked at one another before they retreated to their chairs.

For Cole, the idea of taking her into his arms for dancing, or for any reason, was pure torture. Yes, it was the moment, but he knew he wouldn't ever want to let go.

For Jerica, she longed so much to drape her arms around him, to be close enough to feel the pulse of his body at every level, that it frightened her. She sat down in the rocker and sipped the cooled cider, and he sat down across from her, pretending to be winded from the fast moves.

"That was fun," she said.

"Yeah, well," he began, "maybe for you. I've got five years on you, you know."

"Oh, wow," Jerica said, "shall I fetch you your cane now you poor old thing?"

Cole laughed. "I can tell you'd be cruel to me in my old age. I think I'd better find myself a woman who'll be sweet and sensitive to my needs."

Jerica raised an eyebrow and looked at him. She knew he was kidding, but inside, something felt like pins were being stuck into her heart - she hated the idea that he would have another woman for anything.

She looked up at the clock on the wall. "It's after ten," she said, "I need to get myself out of this comfortable chair and into my car." She stood and took her empty cider cup to the sink. "Thank you for everything," she said as he stood and walked to the sink area next to her.

"You're welcome," he said.

Jerica slipped into her jacket, gave Murphy an ear rubbing, and then looked up at Cole. "See you later."

"Murph and I will walk you to your car," he said.

He held the door open for her and wished she wasn't leaving, not now, not ever. At the car, she unlocked the door and, as before, he opened it and she slid in behind the wheel.

"Before you go," he said, "I want you to know how much I love that driftwood. When I was a kid, my dad and I used to walk the shoreline looking for driftwood to put in our flower gardens and patio area. We always looked at each piece as nature's work of art. That piece you gave to me is particularly nice, and it brought back some great memories."

Jerica looked at his handsome face illuminated by moonlight and a small ship's lantern on a post next to her car.

"I'm glad you like it," she said, and then, reluctantly, they said goodnight.

Chapter Twelve

A few days before Thanksgiving, Cole stopped at his mother's house to leave a wooden box filled with pumpkins. He knew she loved them; she already had four of them guarding the pathway to her front door.

"Where did you get them?" she asked with delight in her voice.

"The basketball coach, Tom Fellows, has a garden full of them. He brought his pick-up truck today, the back overflowing with pumpkins. I took one for my front steps, the rest are yours."

"They're beauties," Mary said. "Oh, by the way, it will be just the four of us for Thanksgiving. I'm starting to get things together. Do you still want to do the dinner preparations with me? I was thinking that being back at school and all, maybe you won't have the time."

"No," Cole said, "I'll be ok with helping, everything's under control. So, who's the four of us? You, Jim, Aunt Jane, and me?"

"No, Jane's going to Helena's house this year. It's you, me, Jim, and Jerica."

Cole's heart felt like it had fallen to the ground. He wanted to ask why, but decided to play it cool and say nothing.

"Okay, sounds good," he said. "We'll confer on who's doing what later this week."

"Great," Mary said. "Now, want a cup of coffee before you head home?"

It was tempting; if he stayed for a while, he'd probably see Jerica.

"No, thanks anyway. I should get home to Murph, and I have a paper to write too. Enjoy your pumpkins. I'll catch up with you later."

On his way home, Cole felt that if he'd been walking instead of driving, his feet would have been off the ground thinking about spending Thanksgiving with Jerica. He wondered why, why she wasn't going to Ohio, or why she wasn't going to be with Dan, but what was most important of all was that she would be with him. The fight he felt within was all about daring to love and lose.

When Jerica arrived home from work it was already dark outside. She walked into Mary's warm and welcoming kitchen and found the wooden box and its contents. "So many pumpkins! They're great, Mary, where did you find them?"

Mary explained that Cole had brought them. "He knows I'm a pumpkin nut," she said. "I've put three from this bunch on the front steps with the original four I'd bought, two at the back door, and I have one or two in every room downstairs, even the bathroom. There must be another dozen here that aren't spoken for, any ideas?"

"Sure," Jerica said as she knelt down to examine and select two from the dozen or so remaining. "I'd love one for my room upstairs and another for my desk at work. Thank you, Mary."

"By the way, Cole and I are going to plan our Thanksgiving meal soon. Would you care to have a voice in the menu? We're pretty traditional, but maybe you have a favorite family recipe or just a fresh idea."

Jerica slipped out of her coat and sat down at the kitchen table. "I'll be out with Dan for a while on Thanksgiving Eve, but when I get in, I'd love to make something either of your choice or mine. Other than that, I think you and Cole should continue to do the meal planning as always. He did delegate me to peeling potatoes, however, if I was going to be here for dinner."

Mary laughed. "You know why? Because that was always his job as a boy and not one he enjoyed."

Jerica nodded and smiled. "I thought it was something like that."

Mary stood and walked to the oven, turning it off. "I have a chicken pot pie and green beans for dinner, Dear. Should be ready in fifteen minutes or so."

"That sounds good," Jerica said. "I'll slip upstairs and change. In fact, would it be completely rude of me to get into pajamas this early? I love my pajamas."

Mary laughed. "You go right ahead. It's one of those raw nights; pajamas would be an excellent idea."

When Jerica went upstairs, Mary thought, as she had many times before, that this was an extremely delightful girl. She smiled and then took the pot pie out of the oven.

On Thanksgiving Eve, Jerica had an early dinner date with Dan. His family had invited her, but she had declined an invitation to fly, in a private plane, to South Carolina, and from there to a friend's private yacht for Thanksgiving. It didn't seem like the place to be for such a holiday, in a tropical atmosphere on the ocean.

"I feel terrible to be leaving you," Dan said. "Are you sure you won't change your mind? We've done this before; it's great out on the yacht, pure luxury."

"I'm glad you're going," Jerica said. "I know you'll enjoy it and it truly isn't for me. Besides, I'll be fine with Mary."

"I wish you were at least going home," he said.

Jerica thought, I am home.

"I don't like you hanging out with that son of hers. There's something irritating about him," Dan said.

Jerica took a deep breath. "It'll be fine, Dan, it's just dinner, that's all. You know why I didn't go to Ohio. With the festivities at my sister's house, it's going to be bedlam. I'd rather visit with my family when I can have them to myself."

Dan still didn't like it, but his choices were limited. Christmas would be different, at least then Jerica would go to Ohio while he and his family went skiing in Utah.

Jerica left Dan soon after seven. He had an hour's drive to meet his family at the airport for their flight to South Carolina, and she wanted to get home where she could prepare some of the next day's meal.

When she arrived at Mary's, Jerica expected to see Cole's car, but there was only Mary's. She unlocked the back door and went into the house where she found a note on the kitchen table.

Dear Jerica,

Cole and I have gone out for a light meal, maybe pizza. He came here at three and it's now six-thirty and we're done! All there is left to do is a couple of the vegetables tomorrow, and whatever you decide to make will be wonderful. I've made the pumpkin pies, so you decide. We should be home around eight.

See you then, Mary.

Jerica swallowed and looked around at the neat kitchen, rich with the pleasant scent of cinnamon and the sweetness of sage for the stuffing. She wished Mary and Cole were there, but she changed into jeans and a jersey, tied an apron around her waist and began to assemble the items she'd purchased to make stuffed mushrooms and a pecan pie.

It proved to be a sentimental evening for her, thinking as she worked about her family. They were surely busy preparing food to take to her sister's home; she'd been told that a total of seventeen people were expected for dinner. She dusted flour off her hands and decided to call her parents. She spoke with her brother and then both her father and mother. Her father joked about being a slave and her mother dismissed his claims. They told her they'd miss her and she told them that she was fine, just busy, and she'd see them at Christmas.

Jerica measured and mixed, washing utensils as she went, the TV on Mary's counter switched on for company. When the kitchen door opened, Jerica was startled until she saw Cole.

"Hey, what are you doing home so early? Mom and I thought you wouldn't get in until later, maybe ten or eleven," Cole said.

"No, Dan had to catch his flight to South Carolina; I've been home since just after seven," she said. "I thought I'd get started on my contribution for tomorrow."

Cole sat down at the kitchen table.

"Where's your mom?" Jerica asked.

"With Jim. We went for a pizza and he was there picking one up to have alone. We ended up sitting and eating together. Jim asked us to see a movie, I declined and Mom accepted. She'll be home around ten or ten-thirty."

Jerica smiled and said, "What do you make of those two? They're spending more and more time together." She gestured to the cup of coffee she'd poured for herself and Cole nodded that he'd have coffee too.

"I think they're two great people, but Mom seems determined to keep it a friendship. She's laid it all out for Jim and he tells her he'd rather have this relationship than none with her, so I don't see things changing. But, that's okay; they're having a good time."

"I agree," she said and then sat down across from him.

"So, are you through with your baking for tomorrow and prepared to eat hearty? Mom has never learned to pare down the portions. We eat leftovers here for a week."

Jerica laughed. "Yes," she said, "and I'm looking forward also to the walk and watching White Christmas."

Cole smiled: she'd remembered. This was definitely the sweetest, prettiest, most charming girl he'd ever known. He finished his coffee then left to go home.

Jerica continued to sit at the table sipping her warm coffee. With the cup nearly drained, she took it to the sink and washed both her cup and Cole's, holding his a bit longer where his hands had been, where his lips had been.

She dried her hands. It was after nine, Mary would be home in another hour or so. Jerica walked slowly through the downstairs rooms, looking at family pictures and other sentimental belongings. She picked up a small silver cup on the living room mantle, the name John Michael on its side. Jerica examined the small item, then placed it back on the mantle and continued to look around. This house was so warm, filled with carefully selected furnishings, some inherited, some purchased. Jerica hoped she'd one day claim a space this special, and then she thought of Cole's home taking shape, him being contemplative about what should go where, like the rocking chair in his kitchen that had once belonged to his grandmother. She wanted that kind of home. Having moved a few times, her parents had often discarded old furniture and replaced it with new to accommodate a different house. Although her environment growing up was attractive and ample, she'd always felt that something was missing. Mary and Cole knew about not letting go of these things that made a house a home, things with a warm history.

By the time Mary came home at ten-twenty, Jerica had walked and wondered her way through the house and was back in the kitchen covering the stuffed mushrooms and pecan pie before making room for them in the refrigerator.

"Hi, Dear," Mary greeted Jerica as she was coming through the kitchen door. "I hope you haven't been alone here all evening. I figured I'd beat you home."

Jerica made room in the packed refrigerator for her food and then turned to Mary and smiled. "I've been home a few hours, but I was fine. I have my pie and mushrooms for tomorrow, and I hope you won't mind my saying, I've been walking around the house, exploring. You and Cole have a knack for integrating warmth; I really love it."

"Thank you," Mary replied. "You explore all you want; I expect you to treat this house as your home. It's not a fancy place, but it's where I most prefer to be."

Jerica nodded. "The little silver cup on the mantle, did that belong to your husband?"

Mary's twinkling eyes softened. "Yes, that was John's, a Christening gift from his grandparents." Mary laughed and continued, "His maternal grandparents gave him that, and, you may have noticed, there's no McGinnis to accompany John Michael. The story goes that the maternal and paternal grandparents weren't that fond of one another and his mother's parents weren't going to add that last name."

"I never thought about your late husband's name," Jerica said, "so it was John Michael McGinnis."

"Yes," Mary nodded, "and Cole's middle name is Michael as well. There were Michaels on each side of our families, so it made good sense."

"It's a nice name," Jerica agreed. "Is there more we should do tonight for tomorrow's dinner, Mary? I wondered about some of the other vegetables."

"No, we're done for now. Cole is peeling potatoes while watching the parade in the morning; that's how we always sweetened the deal when he was younger."

Jerica laughed. "That was sneaky. I think I told you before, Cole told me that I could peel the potatoes if I was around. He made it sound like a privilege."

Mary laughed. "Well of course! He'd love to pass the job off to someone else."

Jerica shook her head and smiled. What could she say? He was charming - she'd peel a palm tree if he asked her to. At least she'd want to, but maybe she wouldn't exhibit such a vulnerable side.

"I think I'll go up to bed then, Mary. I have about twenty pages left of a good book; I'll let it lead me to dreamland."

Mary smiled as she stood to turn off the overhead kitchen light. "Bed sounds good to me too."

"What time is kitchen duty?" Jerica asked.

"Well, I'll get up at five-thirty to get the oven ready," Mary said, but after that, I'll plunk myself down in the recliner and rest until around seven. Most things are done, just a few finishing touches here and there. You sleep as long as you want. When you get up, there will be coffee and cinnamon buns waiting to start the day."

Jerica said goodnight and climbed the stairs to her rooms, feeling both pleased and sad. Being with Mary and Cole was wonderful, but not being with her family made it seem bittersweet. She wondered what they were doing at that moment. Everything was different when the children grew up and went their own ways. With her sister's in-laws now a part of the festivities, it somehow made the day more formal. Jerica wondered if it was just her, being too sentimental over remembered holidays when she was little. Maybe, she thought, I should go to visit them more often. Stretched across her bed, Jerica held a book in her hands. It was hard being divided between people and places. She opened the book and began to read, falling asleep before she could finish the final chapter.

Chapter Thirteen

When Jerica woke up Thanksgiving morning, the sun was struggling through the pines and barren trees, coloring the tiny white specks of falling snow with a blush pink tone. She turned on her side, facing the windows, watching the magic show outside.

She thought about how lucky she was to be in this place, surrounded with good and loving people. She wished again that she hadn't made the decision regarding her career, it was all wrong for her. But then, this job was how she came back to be living in Mystic. And then she thought about Dan. She felt certain that he wasn't the one, but wondered if that was because she was falling in love with someone else. It would be so easy, too easy, to be wrapped up in Cole's life. Although she had many uncertainties in general, her feelings for Cole left her with no doubts. He was incredible. She loved too how his relationship with his mother folded itself around that woman's life like a warm blanket. It had been an old adage of her mother's, how a man treats his mother, so will he treat his wife. Jerica smiled, turned over, and then swung her legs out of bed and put her feet into slippers. The clock said eight-ten. She hurried to the bathroom, back to her bedroom for her robe, and ran downstairs to apologize to Mary for oversleeping.

When she reached the kitchen, her apology halfway out of her mouth, she found Cole and not Mary at the kitchen sink.

"Cole, what are you doing here?"

He gave her a crooked smile, for both her question and her attire. "I brought a couple of things over that I knew Mom would want to put the finishing touches to. And," he said as he held up a mesh sack of potatoes, "look at what I've brought for you."

"You total creep!" she blurted out, and then they both laughed.

"Sorry," she said, "that just slipped out."

Cole laughed again, "Obviously."

"Do you really want me to peel potatoes?" she asked.

"Yup. I hate peeling potatoes."

"Who likes it?" Jerica asked. "All right, I'll do them. I suppose it's the least I can do. Where's your mother? I feel so bad not to have been up earlier."

"Don't worry about it, Mom's used to cooking a big meal, she loves it. She ran over to Deena's with some of her homemade cinnamon rolls. She'll be right back. Want some coffee?"

"Yes, please. Will Deena be joining us for dinner?" she asked as Cole passed her a mug of coffee and she sat down.

"No, Deena has a nephew who lives in New London. He's picking her up later to take her to his house for dinner."

Jerica nodded. "Your mom is so good to her."

"Mom's good to most people. There have been a few she didn't care for, including relatives, but in general, she's pretty cool about things. Well," he said after finishing his coffee, "I'm heading out. I promised Murph a walk on the piers this morning. I'll be back around one. I was told we'd have dinner at three, promptly."

Cole rubbed his hands together and said, "So, little girl, prepare to eat, drink, and be merry."

"And to take a walk and watch White Christmas," Jerica reminded him.

Cole laughed. "Yup, those too."

"Hey," she said, "the parade will be on in a few minutes, I want to see that."

"Good idea. And if you peel the potatoes while watching, it's great. You won't even realize you're peeling potatoes at all."

Jerica stood and put one hand on her left hip. "Oh? So why have you given me the honor?"

He smiled devilishly. "You're just lucky I guess."

Jerica gave him a look and at that point he smiled, waved, and left. She watched him go and then she sat down again to finish her coffee.

She thought about Mary's preparations. The eighteen-pound turkey was in the oven and the aroma was just beginning to tempt. The vegetables were cooked, ready for last minute heating; there was little to do except for the potatoes, which she peeled and cut. With that done, she went back upstairs and changed into jeans and a red jersey, straightened the rooms she used, then went back down to the kitchen. From the window over the sink Jerica could see clusters of Chrysanthemums in shades of rust, gold, bright yellow, and white, all possible victims of that morning's snow and eventual cold. She decided to scoop out the insides of a pumpkin, creating a vase for the pretty fall flowers. After spending an hour cutting and arranging, Jerica left the centerpiece on the kitchen table for Mary to decide where it should be placed.

When Mary walked into the kitchen just past eleven, Jerica was setting her mushrooms on a warming tray in an attractive circular pattern.

"That pumpkin," Mary exclaimed with delight, "is beautiful. Did you do this?" she asked Jerica.

"Yes, I couldn't resist. I hope you don't mind me clipping some of your flowers."

"Absolutely not. I'm thrilled; this is so perfect for our centerpiece today. I'll put it on the dining room table."

"What else can I help with, Mary?"

Mary looked around and said, "I think it's all under control. I see the potatoes are ready. You or Cole?"

Jerica smiled. "They were a gift from Cole to me," she said, "but I softened the chore by watching the parade."

"That devil!" Mary said.

"What do we wear?" Jerica asked. "Dress up or casual like this?" she pointed to her jeans and jersey outfit.

"You look perfectly fine to me, Dear. I wear casual. I'll change out of these things, but I'll be in slacks and a comfy shirt. We're pretty laid back now that we have so few of us at dinner. It's kind of nice I think."

Jerica agreed.

"We'll cook those potatoes just before dinner and then we'll warm everything else in the nice, hot oven while the turkey rests before carving. It's great, isn't it? I love this holiday."

"I do too," Jerica said. "It's so festive, and for me, it's the beginning of Christmas decorating and baking. My mother used to make ginger stars and we'd put little holes in the top of one point. We ate most of them, but the ones that survived the holes and didn't fall apart were adorned with little pieces of embroidery thread and hung on the trees outside for the squirrels."

Mary smiled. "What a great idea. We should do that too. I love the Christmas season as you do; my tree will go up tomorrow. That's part of what Cole does for me. He'll set the tree in its stand and put the lights on it, and later I'll decorate it. Sometime over the weekend, he'll probably put his own up as well. We both have artificial trees, environmentally conscious you know: no trees die for us!"

"I like that idea," Jerica said. "Mom has been doing artificial also; she likes the tree up for a long time so it makes sense. But you're right, it saves a tree."

Mary smiled. "It's twelve-thirty," she said. "Cole is coming around one, Jim at two. Should we have a glass of wine when they're here, maybe with your wonderful stuffed mushrooms?"

"Yes," Jerica said, "that sounds good. And since we're ready except for cooking the potatoes, would you mind if I take a short walk? It's so crisp and beautiful outside, I loved being in the yard cutting the flowers earlier."

"Of course I don't mind, Dear. It is beautiful out, go ahead. I'm going to change into some clean clothes. I was helping Deena root through her attic for a warming tray and I seem to have found the dust. You go, work up a good appetite."

Jerica pulled on a warm jacket and buttoned it against late November's chill. She walked slowly, taking in the glorious flame colors of the trees and watched the birds collecting bits of dried leaves and twigs to insulate their nests.

With each step she took, she mingled her thoughts, her family in Ohio, Dan off with his family on a tropical sail, and Cole. Quicksand, that's what she thought of with each unstable scenario in her life. Ohio didn't seem like home, it never had, and while Mystic did, her job there was far from what she wanted. Then there was Dan. He had expectations for their future together, and yet, Jerica knew in her heart that what she felt for him was not love. What's more, she wasn't so sure that she trusted his commitment, which for her, was vital in a relationship.

After walking for about fifteen minutes, her hands tucked into her jacket pockets, Jerica came upon a stone footbridge, which crossed over a meandering stream. She stopped to watch as golden leaves from a nearby birch tree allowed themselves to be floated away, touching granite rocks and being delayed by the reaching branches. It was peaceful, exciting, and wonderful - this small slice of blue through a slightly toasted landscape. After a good ten minutes there, Jerica turned and headed back to Mary's. It was past one, time for appetizers and wine, and Cole.

"Hey," he greeted her as he uncorked a bottle of wine, "hope you got those potatoes peeled."

Jerica pretended surprise. "Oh, I forgot all about them!"

Cole smiled as he poured four glasses of pale pink liquid. "Yeah, well then, a good fairy did your work for you. I saw the pan full and it's cooking as we speak."

Jerica slipped out of her jacket and hung it on a nearby hook. "Where's your mother?"

"In the dining room with Jim, he showed up a little early. They're putting the final touches to the table. Your pumpkin is taking center stage: very nice."

"Thanks," she said and smiled, then walked into the dining room. "Mary, what can I do to help?"

"Not a thing, Dear. Go say hi to Jim, he's in the living room watching a football game. Cole's getting the wine and mushrooms; we'll wet our whistles before the grand feast."

Dinner was filled with good food and even better conversation. When they'd discussed unrest in the world, careers they'd had or wished they'd had, and family traditions they'd grown up with, Mary asked Jerica where she'd gone on her walk.

"Toward town," Jerica said, "to a beautiful little footbridge over a stream, then back."

Mary looked at Cole. "Sounds like she found your favorite spot."

"Seems so," Cole said. "That's Braeden's Creek. I used to go there to watch for salamanders and to dream. I always wondered if I followed the flow of water, where it would lead me. I imagined to some far off exotic places. Eventually I learned that it leads to the sea."

"And therefore," Jerica said, "to some far off and exotic places, just as you'd thought." The magic she'd felt there at the footbridge was now explained: she'd felt Cole's presence there. Cole gave her a long glance but neither of them said more because anything could seem like too much.

Jim watched the faces of the two young people, sure that they had a sweet bond. Then he looked at Mary, her gentle eyes moving from her much loved son to beautiful Jerica. "Well," he said as he patted his stomach, "who's up for helping me with the dishes? I didn't make a single morsel of this wonderful meal, the least I can do is clean up."

Everyone offered their help and began to gather dishes from the table.

"Wait," Mary said, "I have an idea. Cole, take Jerica down and show her Findlay's, I'll bet she didn't see that part of the creek. Jim and I can take care of the dishes. We'll stack the dishwasher and let some of the pans soak. When you kids get back, maybe we'll be ready for some dessert and coffee."

Jerica protested. "We can't leave all this for you two, that's not fair."

"Now listen," Mary said, "Jim's interested in checking out the football game and we can do that right here in the kitchen. After rooting around in Deena's attic this morning, I'm not all that enthused about our traditional walk. You two go, have a nice stroll, then we can settle in with dessert and White Christmas when you get home."

Cole and Jerica looked at one another.

"What is Findlay's?" Jerica asked.

"Okay," Cole began, "grab your jacket, I'll show you. Jim, don't eat my share of the dessert," he said with a grin.

Jim shook his head. "Can't guarantee that one," he said, "these girls know how to cook."

Cole led Jerica down the street toward the center of town and to the footbridge at Braeden's Creek. "Did you know that Mystic was well known for its ship building capabilities in the sixteen-hundreds? Between the late seventeen hundreds and around nineteen twenty, more than six-hundred vessels were built along the Mystic River. The place was booming. Six generations of the Mallory family were well known for their shipping business to both local and faraway destinations. They were a prosperous family and they brought prosperity to the region."

"I didn't know about the ships," she said. "It's great here, so beautiful, serene."

Cole looked at her and thought he could comment the same about her. "Come on." He urged her down a narrow path alongside the stream. "I'll show you the famed Findlay's Rock."

They arrived at a place where a large boulder sat undisturbed in the middle of the shallow, flowing water.

"This was named for Judson Findlay, a naturalist who sat there often and made some pretty interesting sketches. His work is on many walls around town, and he actually wrote a book about the local offerings of plant life. All the kids around here have been on Findlay's Rock, some got pretty wet getting there, including me."

Jerica smiled. "You have so much to recall of your childhood. It's really wonderful."

"Don't you?" he asked looking at the way her long hair moved in the soft breeze.

Jerica shook her head. "Not like this. I wish I did. We lived in nice neighborhoods, but it was all about houses, no places to wander like you had. I really wish my parents had never left here."

Cole was quiet for a few moments, and then he pointed to a cluster of purple Asters growing on the opposite bank. He glanced at her again, enjoying her sweet profile. "Are you ready to go back?" he asked. "Dessert and White Christmas are waiting."

Jerica smiled and buttoned her jacket to brace herself against the cold. In silence, they walked back to the house and, upon entering, were met by the aroma of fresh coffee and a table laden with desserts.

"Everything's set," Mary said. "The desserts and coffee are out, help yourselves to whatever you'd like, and then we'll put our feet up with the movie. It's in the VCR, ready to go. Jim's never seen it, can you imagine that?"

Cole looked at Jim and said, "You're in for a two-way treat: delicious desserts and a good movie."

"I'm happy to be joining you fine folks," he said. "This has been a truly delightful day."

When the sentimental musical was over, everyone looked prepared for a nap. It was past seven and dark as Jim stood and stretched.

"I can't begin to say how much this has meant today," he began. "Mary, you, Cole and Jerica, have been wonderful companions, and the meal was superb. I thank each one of you from the bottom of my heart."

"Come on," Mary said, "there's plenty of coffee in the kitchen. You can have one more cup for the road. Anyone else for coffee?"

Cole and Jerica declined and stayed lazily in the living room watching the flickering flames in the hearth.

"Are you working tomorrow?" Cole asked her.

"No, I opted to take the day. I like to go out early, have coffee or tea someplace, then go and buy one or two Christmas gifts before the crowds appear. Then I come home. I used to help my mother put up the tree, maybe I'll see about helping your mother to put up hers."

"Good. I'll dig it out tomorrow morning and get the lights on and even. After that, you two can have a great time placing the ornaments in all the right places."

"What about you?" Jerica asked. "You have a tree too, don't you?"

"Yup. Mine is small, three feet high. Someday I'll probably get a big one, something for the corner near the fireplace. For now, the little one is fine. Want to help me decorate it? Maybe on Saturday evening? I'll provide cider and cookies.

Jerica laughed. "Bribery! Yes, I'll help, but the cider needs to be warm and with cinnamon sticks."

"Deal," he said.

With Jim gone by eight, Mary made a quick appearance in the living room to announce her intention for a warm bath and bed with a book.

Cole stood and hugged his mother. "The tree in the morning?" he asked.

"Oh, yes, that would be perfect," she said. "What are your plans, Dear?" she asked Jerica.

"A quick shopping trip. It's been my mother's and my tradition. The day after Thanksgiving, we pick up one or two Christmas gifts, then we get home before the crowds. I could help you with the tree when I get back if you'd like."

Mary smiled. "Great, that would be fun. Maybe Cole will join us for leftovers around noon or one?" she directed the suggestion to him.

"Sure. Hot turkey sandwiches with puddles of gravy? Wouldn't miss it. I'll get the tree up early, then I'll get back to my place; I have a paper to write."

"Good," his mother agreed. "And I'll have a nice package of leftovers ready for you to take home. You can share the turkey with Murphy and the cats: they'll love it."

"How about pie? They like pie too," Cole said with a serious face.

Mary tossed a pillow at her son. "You'll get pie too, unless you eat it all at lunch tomorrow. See you two later."

When she disappeared around the corner toward the bathroom and bedroom, Cole walked to the coat rack by the kitchen door, Jerica followed.

"I should go and let Murph out. I was going to bring him today, but decided he'd be begging us all for treats. He'll get his reward along with the cats; I wrapped a few pieces of turkey up for them, and Mom will send more tomorrow."

Jerica laughed. "What, no sweet potatoes and stuffing?"

Cole smiled. "I'll see you tomorrow. And don't forget, Saturday we trim my tree."

Chapter Fourteen

On Saturday morning, after changing into warm clothes and enjoying an eggs and toast breakfast with Mary, Jerica went back upstairs where she opened bags from Friday's shopping. In Mystic's village she'd found a pewter shop where she had purchased a pretty bread tray for her parents and a small sailboat ornament on a red silk cord for Cole's tree. Around ten o'clock, she went back downstairs and asked Mary if there was anything she might need help with. Mary explained that with the tree now up, decorated, and the house in order, she thought she'd meet two friends for lunch and a little shopping. That evening she was seeing a movie with Jim.

"That sounds nice and relaxing," Jerica said. "I'm going to Cole's to help decorate his tree about four o'clock, but I think I'm spending the rest of the day here, relaxing and wrapping a few gifts."

"Good plan," Mary said, "and if you want a sandwich or something, there's still some turkey, but there are other choices in the deli drawer as well. Help yourself, Dear."

With Mary gone, Jerica washed her hair and bundled it up in a white towel. In the middle of wrapping gifts, Jerica decided to call her parents to see how their Thanksgiving was and how they were.

"It was busy," her mother said. "I like the whole bunch, but it's like attending a very noisy party."

Jerica laughed. "I know: that's why I decided to stay here this time. For Christmas, we'll just stay by ourselves, right?"

There was a hesitation from her mother.

100

Jerica waited and then said, "Mom, are you still there?"

"Yes, I'm sorry, Jerica. I'm trying to figure out how to say this without sounding like I don't want to see you at Christmas. I'm afraid there might be a change this year. I know you planned on coming out here to Ohio, but your father and I might not be here."

"Why?" Jerica said with almost a gasp in her voice.

"It's the Gilpens - Paula and Ken. They had tickets to go to Hawaii for the holidays but now there's a medical problem with Paula's mother and they can't go. They've offered the tickets and accommodations to us free. We'll give them something, of course, but it's an unusual opportunity. Would you be terribly upset if we went?"

Jerica swallowed and then said, "No, of course not. If this is something you and Dad would enjoy, it sounds great. What about Sharyn and her family, and Brandon? What will they do?"

"Well," Jerica's mother began, "Sharyn will go to her in-laws', and Brandon may go there too. He has a girlfriend now, so he might opt for going with her family. It's you I'm concerned about. Sweetheart. I'd hoped to see you."

Jerica felt her eyes brim with tears. "It's okay," she said, "I'll visit you after the holidays. It'll be less hectic that way. You go on that trip and have fun. Take lots of pictures and send me some."

"Oh, we will," her mother's voice sounded lighter with the feared subject off her mind.

"I'm wondering about gifts," Jerica said. "Should I mail them or just wait until I visit later?"

"Let's do that," her mother said. "I'll keep my little tree up until you get here, and then we'll celebrate with a nice dinner and our gifts to one another."

After Jerica had said goodbye, she sat on her bed and cried. Had it been so easy to put her away from their lives? It occurred to her that maybe it was her fault, after all, she's the one who'd moved away. Now she wasn't certain what to tell Mary, or Dan. Jerica knew that skiing in Utah was not going to be for her, and yet, she didn't want to infringe on Mary and Cole's Christmas plans either. Maybe she'd go off on her own, but to where? It all seemed a little sad, but she reminded herself that at the hospital where she worked, there were many who were very sick and even dying. She wanted to be glad that everyone close to her was well. And then she thought that maybe she'd spend time at the hospital on Christmas, volunteering in some way.

At four, Jerica left Mary's home with the little pewter ornament for Cole and drove to his house. She found him outside on a ladder cleaning the fallen leaves out of his roof's gutter. "Don't tell me I have to navigate that height to decorate your tree," she greeted him.

Cole looked down and smiled. "Oh, yeah, didn't I explain that part to you?"

Murphy danced at the foot of the ladder, half because he was anxious about where his friend was working and half because he was happy to see Jerica.

"Go ahead in," Cole suggested, "and take that worry-wart with you. He's been whining the whole time I've been up on this ladder."

"All right, how long before you'll be in?"

"Give me another ten minutes," Cole said, "by then, I'll be ready for a warm drink and decorating the tree."

Jerica urged Murphy into the house where she filled his water bowl and offered him a milk bone from a jar on the counter. "There you go," she spoke to the dog and patted his shoulders. She looked around the cozy kitchen and said, "Okay, there's coffee all made, but maybe I'll warm some cider too. What do you think, Murphy?"

The dog barked and she laughed. "Good answer," she said.

When Cole came in and slipped out of his plaid flannel shirt revealing the dark green jersey underneath, Jerica couldn't help but notice the firm physique. He was incredibly handsome.

"Smells good in here," he commented, "what did you do?"

"It's the cider," Jerica said, "I hope you don't mind. I heated some with a bit of cinnamon."

Cole nodded, but he was thinking how warm and comforting it was, coming into his loved home to such a scene and the pleasant aroma. This was what he wanted.

"So, where's the tree?" Jerica asked as she poured two mugs of cider and passed one to Cole.

"In the living room," he said, "but knowing how much you like this kitchen, I'm wondering if we should move it in here."

Jerica felt a pang in her heart that he would consider her in that manner.

"What do you think?" he asked when she'd said nothing.

"Well, what would you think of having a tiny tree in the kitchen? I used to have one in my bedroom when I was growing up; it was just about one foot high. It had little white lights and I cut white stars to decorate it with. It was very cute."

Cole pursed his lips and nodded. "I like that idea. So I'll pick up a little tree and lights this week, and you can cut me some of those little stars, deal?"

Jerica laughed. "Sure, I'll do the stars." What wouldn't she do for him? She couldn't think of a thing.

When they'd finished their cider, Cole led Jerica into the living room. He'd placed the three-foot high tree on top of an old trunk; its lights were small, white, and incredibly magical.

"This is my box of ornaments," he said as he moved the lid on a square cardboard carton. "Most of them belonged to my grandparents."

"They're wonderful," Jerica said, and then she remembered the pewter sailboat in her purse and went into the kitchen for it. When she returned, she handed it to him wrapped in tissue.

"What's this?" he asked as he unwrapped the paper, revealing the small vessel. "Wow," he said, "this is beautiful. For me?"

"Sort of," she said with a smile, "I do think it would look best on the tree though."

Cole looked at her for several moments before turning to hang it front and center on his tree. "Okay, we're done," he announced.

Jerica laughed. "Oh, no you don't! Come on, let's hang these pretty ornaments, this is going to be the best tree in town."

With Christmas carols playing in the background, they hung the last ornament and placed a slightly tattered star on the tree top, and then they stood back and to admire the soft glow.

"There's nothing more beautiful than a Christmas tree," Jerica said.

Cole looked at her, thinking that Jerica was more beautiful than any Christmas tree he could imagine. He abruptly changed the subject, "Are you hungry?" he asked. "It's nearly six, I'm starving."

"I could eat," Jerica said. "Should we go out for something? Or if you have plans, I can go back to your mom's and have something."

"I have no other plans. We can go out, or I can pick us up something. What do you feel like having?"

"Pizza," Jerica replied. "We could have pizza in by the tree."

"You've got it," he agreed. "I'll call it in and pick it up. Your job is to feed Murphy and the cats while I'm gone. How's that for a plan?"

"Sounds agreeable," Jerica said as she moved toward the kitchen with Murphy leading the way.

While Cole was gone, she fed the pets and looked around the kitchen from her rocking chair vantage point. It was warm and inviting and filled with Cole. She thought about Christmas and tears came to her eyes. As an adult, she understood her parents' decision to go away on a wonderful trip, but as their daughter, she felt slightly abandoned and misplaced.

When Cole walked in carrying the pizza, he noticed the moist and red eyes on this beautiful girl. "What's wrong?" he asked.

Jerica smiled. "Nothing. I had a bit of dust in my eyes I guess."

He let it go; she didn't seem to want to share her emotions at that point. They ate by the tree, enjoying its beauty and just being together in the same room.

"So," he said, "when will you go back to Ohio for Christmas? We should have a little dinner, you, Mom, Jim and me, before you go."

Jerica swallowed back tears but was not totally successful.

"Hey," he said, "what's going on here? What's wrong, Jerica?"

She wiped her eyes with a napkin. "Oh, I'm just being sentimental. Mom and Dad are going on a trip to Hawaii over Christmas, so there's no point going to Ohio. I'll go later, maybe in January, I don't know."

Cole felt sad for her. He could see that this was a disappointment. "Well, you'll have Christmas with us then," he said. "Mom said you weren't interested in going skiing in Utah, so stay here with us."

It seemed like such a natural thing for her to do, stay with Cole and Mary, but she also wondered if it was too much of an intrusion.

"I'm not sure," she said. "I was thinking I might go to the hospital that day. I could read to someone or talk to someone who has no family nearby. I'll figure something out."

"Look," Cole said, "you go to the hospital for a few hours if you want, that's a nice idea, but then you come back here for Christmas dinner."

"Here?" she asked.

"Yup. Mom and I agreed: she had Thanksgiving, I get Christmas. Jim will come by later for dessert; he's having dinner with his daughter and her family."

"Okay," Jerica said softly, "thank you, Cole."

He reached over to pat her hand but found himself leaving it there for longer than he'd intended. When they began to notice the warmth being generated, each one moved their hand ever so slightly, and then Cole remembered to remove his hand completely.

When Jerica went home around nine, she found Mary was still out. She plugged in the Christmas tree and turned on two other small lights then went to look for white paper and scissors. By the time Mary came through the kitchen door at nearly eleven, Jerica had cut her twentieth star and was dipping it in glue and white glitter. Mary smiled at the sweet endeavor and explanation. The stars were left to dry on the kitchen table as the two decided to sit by the tree and watch the news before going off to bed.

Chapter Fifteen

On December tenth Jerica received a phone call from her sister inviting her for Christmas. "We'd love to include you," Sharyn said. "You know you're always welcome here. Brandon will stop by at some point, but he has this new girlfriend now and he plans to spend some time with her and her family."

"It's hard to think of Brandon in a serious relationship," Jerica said with a smile, "he's always been our baby brother."

Sharyn laughed. "I know, but he's completely taken by this girl; I guess the love bug really bit this time."

"I guess so. Well, about Christmas, I appreciate the offer and invitation, but I think I'll stay here and visit when Mom and Dad are back. I'm dying to see your little Emmy too; she must be getting so big."

Their conversation went on for another few minutes, catching up on family, in both Ohio and Connecticut; Jerica admitted that she wished for closer contact.

By the way," Sharyn said, "I haven't mentioned anything to Mom and Dad yet and I won't until after the holidays, but there's a strong possibility that we'll be making a move to North Carolina in the spring."

Jerica felt stunned. "Why?" she asked with surprise in her voice.

"A great job offer, and it's beautiful there. I'm excited by it all, but I'm dreading telling Mom and Dad. I'm wondering if they'll move back to Connecticut then, they've always talked about it."

Jerica swallowed hard. "Wow, I'm surprised with all this news, but it sounds like a wonderful opportunity. Have you been to North Carolina to check things out?"

"Yes, we only went for a few days, and we kind of kept it from both sets of parents until we knew if we'd consider it, but we loved it. We'd buy a house there big enough to have everyone come and visit; it could be a lot of fun."

"It sounds nice," Jerica said. "I'd love to visit you and see the area."

When the call ended, Jerica sat down and thought about all that had been said.

Mary entered the kitchen and found Jerica sitting motionless; she looked at the young woman and then asked, "Is everything all right, Dear?"

Jerica looked up at Mary as if coming out of a daze. "Yes, well, that was my sister. She hasn't told Mom and Dad yet, but she and her husband and baby daughter are planning a move to North Carolina. I'm surprised: he's quite close to his family. Like you and Cole, they've always lived in one place; this will be a significant change."

Mary nodded. "I'm sure it will be. I'm making a cup of tea, would you like some?"

"Yes," Jerica said, "that sounds good."

"Your folks will miss that baby grandchild," Mary said. "Moving can be so disruptive."

"I know," Jerica said, "I wish we'd never left Mystic."

"Do you hope to stay here?" Mary asked as she prepared the tea. "I mean, will your Dan be content in a small town like this?"

"I don't know," she said, knowing that Dan would never settle in Mystic. "I guess time will tell."

The two women shared their tea together and spoke of Jerica's work and other subjects. "So," Mary began, "I understand you'll be staying here for Christmas. I'm sorry for those who'll miss you, but I'm awfully glad for us. It'll be wonderful having you, Dear."

"I'm glad too, Mary, thank you. I'm very lucky to have you and Cole. He said dinner would be at his home."

Mary smiled. "Yes, and I'm loving it. He's going to barbeque steaks, and he's doing baked potatoes and salad. I'm making some buttermilk biscuits and a couple of desserts. He loves cheesecake and brownies, so I guess I'll do those."

"I'm getting hungry just thinking about it," Jerica said. "What can I do?"

Mary looked thoughtful. "Hmm, let me think. What about a vegetable dip? Or, I know. You could make Christmas breakfast, your wonderful French Pancakes."

"I'll do both," Jerica said, "I'd love that."

Mary smiled and nodded. "Fine idea."

"What about Jim and other family members or friends?" Jerica asked.

"Well, my sister goes to her daughter's, Jim is going to his daughter's, but he'll stop by later for dessert. That's it," she gestured with her hands out to the side. "We once had big holiday gatherings, but people go their own way and now it's just us. But, I have to admit, I love it, it's almost nicer without all the fuss. My kitchen windows used to be dripping with steam from all the cooking on Christmas, now it's just grilled steak, keeping it simple."

Jerica agreed. "It does sound wonderful, Mary. I'm looking forward to it so much."

Mary offered more tea and a cookie to go with it. "Of course," Jerica accepted, "your peanut butter cookies are irresistible. I have to be careful not to overdo, I enjoy sweets."

Mary smiled, "Me too. The difference is, you're young and slim and I'm not!"

Jerica laughed. "Well, if I want to stay slim, I'll need to take it easy on your good cooking." She took a bite from a thick, delicious cookie, enjoying its rich, buttery taste. After a sip of hot tea she asked, "What about gifts? I'd like to find things that you and Cole would like and something for Jim as well."

Mary munched on a cookie then swallowed and sipped her tea. "I've bought a new watch for Cole, which he needed, and a nice, warm sweater. I bought a warm scarf and gloves for Jim, and they'll both get boxes of cookies. I'm sure they'd love anything, Jerica. As for me, I think I remember you joking about getting me a toy. I'm still four at Christmas time you know!"

Jerica laughed. "Okay, I'll find things; it'll be fun. I love to shop for people I care about."

"Me too," Mary said, "and I found just what I wanted for everyone this year, including you!"

"Oh, what is it?" Jerica asked with an enthusiastic smile.

Mary laughed. "Oh, no. You're not getting it out of me until Christmas."

Jerica smiled and sipped her tea. "So, what's happening between you and Jim? Any possibility you'll consider getting serious with him?"

Mary shook her head vigorously. "No way! Things are different today, kind of like fashion. Years back when John and I married, that was it. It was the only accepted way. Just like wearing a skirt or dress instead of pantsuits and jeans. I can love Jim, and I do, but not in the way I loved John. I don't want the responsibility of marriage now, I like what I have: complete freedom. Jim could bring me a chocolate angel food cake and a Snickers Bar and I still wouldn't say I do."

Jerica nodded and smiled. "I hear you," she said.

"What about you?" Mary asked. "Is marriage what you want? Children?"

Jerica looked thoughtful. "I think so," she said, "but I'm not so sure it's Dan. Actually, I'm pretty certain it's not Dan."

"Really?" Mary asked.

Jerica nodded. "I think most people who know me think that Dan and I are an item, but we're so different. I truly can't see us sharing a life."

Mary was silent for a few moments then said, "You're young, Dear. If Dan isn't the one, someone else will be. I can't see a lovely young woman like you ever ending up alone. You're very special to me, just in case you didn't know that by now."

Jerica's eyes misted. "Thank you, and I feel the same about you and Cole."

That weekend, Jerica went out with Dan who insisted they journey into New York for theatre and dining. She loved that old and vibrant city, especially dressed in holiday cheer, but the further she found herself from Mystic, the lonelier she felt.

In New York, Dan saw a jacket he liked and Jerica offered to buy it for him as a Christmas gift. He wanted her to choose a ring or other piece of jewelry, but she chose instead a pair of knee-high boots in a deep brown color. So, that was that, Christmas for one another was practical and finished. He would leave for skiing in Utah the following weekend and would be gone for two weeks. Jerica felt bad that she didn't care, she was grateful not to have to spend time with him and his family at Christmas.

When Dan left for Utah the following Saturday, Jerica decided to go out and shop for gifts to give Mary, Cole, and Jim. She also purchased several boxes of candy, hand lotion, and powder, to take with her on Christmas to the hospital. She'd teased Mary about getting her a toy since she felt like four at Christmas, and when she found a soft, sweet-faced teddy bear in butterscotch plush, wearing a big red bow, she knew this was the right gift. For Jim, Jerica found a tweed cap, similar to the type he often wore, and for Cole, she purchased a thick and soft navy blue throw for sitting around on cold winter nights. A quick stop at the pet supply store for cat and dog treats and her shopping was complete.

"Goodness," Mary proclaimed as Jerica struggled into the house with her packages. "Did you buy out Mystic?"

Jerica smiled. "Not quite, but I do think I have what I need. I love this time of year. I become aware of what's in the shops. The rest of the year, unless I need new shoes or something, I'm really not much of a shopper."

"Good for you," Mary said, "I'm a little too fond of it I'm afraid. I have a real problem resisting candles and candleholders. My motto is, never enough!"

Jerica laughed. "Well, maybe you're right. Candles are sometimes necessary and always charming."

"That's true," Mary said.

"I can't believe that Christmas is just one week away," Jerica said. "I'm really excited by it this year. I was wondering," she continued, "how I can best blend into your schedule. I thought I'd visit people at the hospital for a few hours, but I can work that around what you and Cole have planned for the day."

"Great," Mary said. "How about if we have some breakfast around eight, your very good pancakes, and after that, you go for your hospital visit. When you come home, you can put your veggie dip together if you wish, then we can go to Cole's for dinner and gifts."

Jerica liked that idea. "So, would it be alright for me to go from maybe ten until two or three?"

"Perfect," Mary said. "We usually do dinner around four, then gifts by the fire. Jim should be there by five or so, and we'll have coffee and dessert with him. It makes for a cozy evening, peaceful and yet festive. I love it."

Jerica nodded, she loved it too, especially this year, in Mystic with Mary and Cole.

Chapter Sixteen

Three days before Christmas snow fell from the skies with a determination to cover everything outside with white. Trees were both burdened and beautiful, all roof tops and other surfaces agreed with one another in creating a monotone palette; it was a serenely wonderful welcome to the Christmas season.

Jerica pulled a warm purple scarf around her slender neck and tugged matching gloves onto her hands before leaving Mary's house for work.

"You look so pretty," Mary said, "that gray coat with the purple accessories is very becoming."

Jerica smiled. "Thanks, Mary. I've had the coat since high school, but the gloves and scarf were a gift from my sister last Christmas."

"Be careful, Dear, the roads could be slick. They look well plowed, but you never know when you could hit an icy patch."

"I'll be careful," Jerica said with a smile. "You're lucky that they canceled school for today."

Mary smiled. "I'm loving it. I plan to make a nice meal for this evening, and I'm going to take this chance to read by the Christmas tree. I wish you could enjoy the day at home too. Maybe I'll give Cole a call later to see if he wants to come for dinner; he's probably going to use this time to do some of his graduate work. Apparently he's taking a literature course next semester and has quite a list of novels to read – that's Cole, getting a head start."

Jerica hesitated at the door, wishing that she didn't have to leave – snuggling in with a book sounded so good on this snowy day. But knowing that she had an important meeting, she begrudgingly went off to the hospital.

When early evening and darkness had converted the snowfall to blue-gray, Jerica pulled into Mary's driveway and found Cole's car there. She maneuvered into her space next to where he'd parked and smiled at the prospect of seeing him.

"Look who's here," he said as she walked into the kitchen brushing snow from her hair. He lifted a pan of cornbread from the oven and set it to cool on the pale granite counter, then smiled at her.

Pulling her scarf and gloves off then unbuttoning her coat, Jerica looked at him and said, "Don't tell me you made that."

"Okay," he said, "I won't. Mom made it. I'm just the gopher here. She made a beef stew to go with this, and I couldn't resist the invitation. These days, I seem to consume an awful lot of pizza."

Jerica smiled. "But you like pizza. I think I'd eat pizza two or three times a week if it weren't for the fact that I need to think healthier."

Cole smiled, his hands on his hips. "Yup, I hear you. But, at least it's better than eating my weight in brownies. Mom's changing her clothes; she'll be right out to join us for supper. Do you need to change or anything before we have our meal? Would you like a glass of wine?"

Jerica hung her coat, stuffing the scarf and gloves into its pockets. "No to both," she said with a smile. "It smells so good in here, I can't wait to eat. I was busy today and bought myself an apple at the cafeteria to munch at my desk. Did you have a nice day at home?"

Cole sat down at the kitchen table to wait for his mother to join them; Jerica followed suit. "Yeah, it was nice. I did a few things around the house, started in on a book for next semester, and plowed out Mom's and my driveway. Murph thought it would be fun to romp in the snow, so we did that too. And, here I am."

Jerica smiled. "It sounds so much nicer than my day. I'm jealous."

Cole looked at her as his mother entered the kitchen wearing jeans and a long-sleeved, cream-colored jersey. "This is nice," she said, "all of us home, together and safe. Let's get this food on the table. You two must be starved."

After their hearty meal and Mary's offer of cookies with freshly brewed coffee, Cole took his plate to the sink and then reached for his jacket. "This has been great," he said, "but I need to get back. Murph will want another trip outside and I should use that time to get the steps in better shape; they were a little slippery when I was leaving the house earlier."

"The roads could be glazed over too, Honey, be careful," Mary said as she patted his back.

He hugged his mother, thought about hugging Jerica, but gave her a look and a smile instead, then left. She stared at the closed door for a few moments, noticed by Mary, who turned away and smiled to herself. With the dishes soaking in hot, soapy water, Mary offered Jerica another cup of coffee or something else to drink.

"I think I won't," Jerica said. "I'd so love a warm bath. Would you mind if I do that after we wash dishes? I could come back down if you'd like the company, or I could just read. What are you doing with the rest of the evening?"

Mary started to wash the dishes. "I'm up for whatever," she said. "But you go ahead and take your bath. There are so few dishes here I'll take care of them. After I'm through, I'll probably go back into the living room to read, watch TV, or just enjoy the tree. If you feel like coming down after your soak, come on down. If you feel like being cozy in your own rooms, you can do that too. You've had a long day at work, you decide, I'll be perfectly fine either way." Mary turned to hug Jerica. "That's in case you choose to stay upstairs," she said.

Jerica took a long, hot bath then pulled on warm flannel pajamas before going to her room. The bed looked so inviting that she plopped down on it and curled into a fetal position where she fell asleep. Sometime during the night she woke and felt chilled, and at that point, she pulled the covers back and slipped beneath them to return to sleep and dreams spun with fragments of an unreachable Cole.

On Christmas Eve, Jerica's parents surprised her with a telephone call from their hotel in Hawaii. "I feel so lonely for you, Sweetheart," her mother said with a quiver in her voice. "Do you have some nice plans with Mary McGinnis and her family?"

"I do," Jerica said. "Don't worry about it, Mom, I'm really fine. We'll have a nice get-together when you're settled back home. How's the weather there? It must be beautiful."

"It is. The weather is bright and sunny, we're actually taking a little tour today, and tomorrow we're having Christmas dinner on a boat. Can you imagine such a thing? Your father is very excited about that. It will be different, but wonderful, I'm sure. We've already met some interesting folks who are here from Pennsylvania, and we expect to see them later today and have dinner with them tomorrow."

They spoke for another ten minutes about Jerica's plans for Christmas and about Sharyn and Brandon. It was a change this year, but everyone was well and that was the major consideration for everything.

At six-thirty, Jerica placed the phone back on its receiver, glad to have talked with her parents. Mary walked into the kitchen where Jerica stood looking reflective and asked if all was okay. "Yes, everything is fine. Mom and Dad called from Hawaii and they're loving it there. I felt sad when they first told me they were going, but now I'm actually happy. This isn't like something they'd ever plan and it's a great opportunity for them to see that beautiful part of the world. And I'm here, with you and Cole. How much better could it be?"

Mary gave her a big hug. "Merry Christmas, Jerica," she said, "I can't tell you how much I love having you with us."

Before midnight, Cole came to pick up his mother for church services; Jerica had been undecided about going with them. When he arrived and stepped in out of the cold, Jerica was there, wearing a dress of brilliant red as she slipped her arms into a black wool coat.

"Well," he said appraising her from head to toe, "you look a lot like a Christmas ornament in that outfit."

"Is it too bright?" she asked, hesitating at buttoning the coat.

"No way," he said. "You look terrific. I take it you're coming with us to church."

"Yes, I decided I would. Your mother has promised hot cocoa when we return."

Cole smiled. "It doesn't take much to persuade you, does it? "

Mary walked into the kitchen, pulling gloves onto her hands, and then they went out to Cole's warm car and drove off for services and midnight carols. It was, Jerica decided, one of the most celebratory Christmases she'd ever known. The candles at the church windows provided the only light and garlands of green princess pine tied at intervals with large red bows set the peaceful yet festive mood. Cocoa and cookies were offered at home and then they said their goodnights. At the archway of Mary's kitchen and dining room, she'd hung a small bouquet of mistletoe. When Mary had gone to hang her coat in the front hall closet, Cole and Jerica were directly beneath the greenery, where he planted a light kiss against her available lips. He pulled away to look at her for a reaction, and when he found no resistance, he took her into his arms and gave her a more thorough and lasting kiss. "There," he said, "Merry Christmas." When he turned and left, Jerica stood there in that special place, her finger tips against her closed mouth, her eyes on the door he'd just closed behind him.

When she awoke on Christmas morning, Jerica could see a golden sun glistening on the snow-covered world outside. She turned more onto her side and stared out at the beauty of the day, thinking that on Christmas especially the sun seemed to take on its own unique glimmer. It was after seven and she had promised to make breakfast, her French Pancakes, which Mary had not yet tasted. Jerica smiled, she loved preparing something special for people she loved and, with that thought, she could envision her parents sitting on some luxurious boat later that day, enjoying something tropical to eat and sipping at Piña Coladas. She swung her long legs out of bed and stretched, then stood and pulled the covers up into place. Discarding the pajamas, she pulled on jeans with a dark green sweater. With bare feet, she practically skipped downstairs and into the kitchen where Mary sat with a cup of coffee and a jar of buttons.

"Merry Christmas," Jerica said as she gave Mary a hug. "What are you doing with those buttons?"

Mary wished Jerica a Merry Christmas and then explained that she was looking for a button to sew on one of her flannel shirts. "I keep these things handy," she said, "you never know when you'll need a button. Cole always teases me about being a keeper of unnecessary objects. John used to do the same thing. But many a time I used this old jar of buttons to fix one of their favorite shirts. Here's what I need," she said with a smile, "this green button will do just fine on my old flannel plaid. Good, I'll sew that on later. Want some coffee, Dear?"

"I'd love it," Jerica said, "I'll get it and I'm going to start making the pancakes if that's all right with you. Is Cole coming for breakfast?"

"Is there water in the ocean?" Mary asked with raised eyebrows. "That boy heard you were making those pancakes and asked what time. He'll be here."

"Should we call him?" Jerica asked with a smile.

"Already did," Mary said, "just as soon as I heard you moving around upstairs. He'll be here shortly."

Jerica poured herself a small cup of coffee, stirring cream and sugar into it, then she took a sip before beginning to assemble the needed ingredients. "You'll like these, Mary, they're so simple, but there's just something so satisfying about them," she said as she broke five eggs into a small bowl for whisking.

"I can't wait," Mary said, "Cole loves them; he's been waiting for another batch to happen along. Is there anything I can do? Would you like some fruit to go with them? I have nice green apples, some oranges I can slice, grapes, whatever you think."

Jerica stopped what she was doing and looked at Mary. "All three sound wonderful. How about just a bit of everything? It would be so festive for Christmas morning breakfast."

"Great idea," Mary said, "I'll cut up one apple, one orange, and a handful of red grapes."

"Is Jim coming?" Jerica asked.

"No, he's leaving around ten for his daughter's house. He'll drop by Cole's later for dessert and coffee."

"He's such a nice man," Jerica commented as she mixed.

Mary gave the young woman a sideways glance. "Yes, he is," she said and then they spoke no more of Jim. Jerica smiled to herself thinking about Mary's independence. She admired her for that: a woman who wasn't compromising but sticking to her feelings and having confidence in being on her own.

Moments later, Cole walked into the kitchen bringing with him a draft of cold air and an excited retriever.

"Murphy," Mary said. "Merry Christmas, Murphy. Let me see what I can give you for a special treat." She looked in the refrigerator and took a small piece of roast beef, which she broke into three tiny pieces. "There you are, Murphy my boy," she said, and then she hugged her son.

"What do you think of a mother who tends to the dog before her son?" he asked Jerica as he hung his coat on the hook by the door.

"I'd say she has her priorities straight," Jerica said with a smile.

Cole put his hands on his hips and looked at her. "Great, I get the distinct feeling I'm being ganged up on here. And on Christmas."

"Could I offer you some cheese with that whine?" Mary asked.

As Jerica spooned pancakes onto the griddle, it took only minutes before the fast cooking delights were being turned and moved to a platter with offerings of butter and salt. "Dig in," Jerica suggested as she continued to cook. Mary served the fruit in a pretty red glass dish and Cole poured coffee into three cups. Within a short time, they were all seated and enjoying their food. Even Murphy was given a pancake, minus the butter and salt.

At ten Jerica gathered her hospital gifts together and went off to spend a few hours with those not fortunate enough to have family nearby or at all. Cole watched her go, thinking what a considerate human being she was, certainly not the run of the mill kind of girl. With Murphy in reluctant tow, Cole left to go home where he would tidy the house for his guests later in the day. "Around four then, Mom. I'll see you later," he said as he gave her a squeeze.

At the hospital Jerica was told which patients might enjoy a visit. There were five who seemed to have no one coming that day, which Jerica found extremely sad. One elderly man was Jewish, but when told about the pretty young woman's quest, he told a nurse he'd like her to stop by to see him as well. Jerica walked into his room with a brightly wrapped package and smiled as she sat down on the chair next to his bed.

"Hi, Mr. Epstein. I'm Jerica Gates, it's so nice to meet you," she said.

He put out his thin hand to her and she took it. "You're a lovely sight for these old eyes," he said. "But what are you doing here on Christmas Day?"

"Visiting," Jerica said with a smile. "I couldn't be with my family in Ohio, so I am spending the holidays with good friends. I thought I'd also like to come here to the hospital to visit."

"Well," he said, "that's very nice of you indeed. What is it that you do with your life?" he asked.

"Actually," Jerica began, "I work here at the hospital, in administration."

The old man looked at her with twinkling blue eyes. "You don't look like the administrative type," he said with a smile.

Jerica placed the gift on his bed next to his hand. "You're right. I'm not in a job I truly like. I've been thinking about what I might consider. Do you have any suggestions?"

"Well," he said with a shaky voice, "you're a good hand holder. How about if you become a nurse?"

Jerica laughed. "Maybe," she said, "I'll have to give that some thought. How about if we open your present?"

"I get one even though I'm an old Jew?" he asked with a smile.

"Absolutely," Jerica replied, "and you're not so old. Let me help to untie that ribbon."

The gift was a small-framed picture of Mystic Seaport, a bag of brightly colored gumdrops, and a small container of talcum powder.

"Oh, my," he said, "how wonderful. Thank you so much, My Dear."

Jerica stayed with Mr. Epstein for nearly one hour, then she moved on to visit the others. Each person was very grateful for the visit and the brightly packaged little gifts. In the end, Jerica felt that she'd received far more than she had given.

Back at Mary's, just before three o'clock, Jerica changed her clothes, deciding to wear a garnet colored dress with shoes to match. With gifts from them both loaded in the car with the vegetable tray and dip, she accompanied Mary and her desserts to Cole's home. From outside, they could hear Christmas Carols and Mary looked at Jerica with a smile. "He does these things - hooks up speakers so that before you ever get inside, you're in the proper mood."

"Well it works, this is magical," Jerica said. "We have snow on the ground and music in the air. It's a perfect Christmas Day."

As they walked through the door, Murphy greeted them with his light woof and wagging tail. Cole was there too, ready to take their coats and contributions to the meal.

"This place looks so festive, Honey," Mary said as Cole leaned forward to kiss her. "And the fire, oh, it smells so nice in here."

He and Jerica exchanged smiles, then she moved closer to give him a hug. "Thank you for this," she said, "it's amazing. I don't think I've ever felt more Christmas-y."

"Then I'll try hard not to burn the steaks," he said as he smiled and took her coat. "I'd hate to ruin your day."

"You can't," she said, "it's already everything I could wish for."

Cole wanted to reach out and grab her, but instead he hung her coat and his mother's, then he offered them a warm brandy or a glass of wine by the blazing living room hearth.

"What are you burning in here?" Mary asked as Cole and Jerica joined her in comfortable living room chairs. "It's so aromatic, it's wonderful."

Cole smiled. "It's actually plain old oak, but I threw some balsam chips in there too and they're like adding salt to stew. Nice, isn't it?"

"Fantastic," Mary said as she sipped the warmed brandy.

Jerica sat back in her roomy chair balancing her glass of deep red wine very carefully. The atmosphere couldn't have been better. Murphy lay at Cole's feet and Edgar, the male tabby, positioned himself on the sofa next to Mary. They talked about Christmases past and amusing happenings by a few eccentric family members. "I have this one cousin," Mary said, "who gets the hiccups about two bites into his meal. We've listened to that go on for literally hours sometimes, until often, a few of us, Cole and I included, would end up in the kitchen where we could dissolve into laughter without being rude."

"And don't forget Aunt Dee," Cole said.

Mary put her hand over her eyes for a moment and laughed. Jerica looked from one to the other, waiting for the punch line.

"You tell her," Mary said snickering, "I'll spill this nice brandy if I try."

Cole laughed then focused his attention on Jerica. "Let's just say that Aunt Dee is quite unusual. She's Mom's aunt, eight-eight spunky years of age at this point. Thankfully, she lives in Florida year round now, but she used to show up at Mom's for Christmas dinner wearing a strapless evening dress and fluffy slippers. Wouldn't have been so bad," he said, "but nothing matched."

Mary burst into gales of laughter, which brought tears to her eyes. Jerica laughed at Mary's reaction more than Aunt Dee's antics, although it was interesting to imagine.

"It sounds like you had very colorful holidays," Jerica said smiling.

Cole shook his head. "That's for sure. Honestly though, I prefer what we have today."

When Jim arrived for dessert and gifts, they opted to have sweets first and then the presents in by the living room fire.

With his new, soft throw over one arm, Cole locked at Jerica and said, "This will be great to snuggle up with on cold Mystic nights. Thank you."

When it was her turn to open Cole's gift to her, Jerica held two presents, one in a ten-inch square box, the other in a tiny black velvet pouch tied with a red satin ribbon. Carefully, she pulled the wrapping from the larger package, revealing a music box in the form of a perfect little merry-go-round. She held it up and turned its switch on to hear the tinkling sweet sound of a familiar waltz. She looked at Cole and hoped traitorous tears wouldn't fall. "Thank you," she managed to say, "this is incredible."

"We have one of the oldest carousels anywhere here in Mystic," he said. "Someday I'll take you there; it's inside where it can be protected from the weather and salt air."

"Okay," she said softly.

"What's in that little pouch?" Jim asked. "Let's see what else you have there from Cole. He's done a good job so far."

Jerica untied the narrow ribbon and opened the velvet piece to find a necklace, a simple sterling silver chain embracing a perfect little silver shell. Jerica opened her mouth to speak, but nothing came out.

"That's lovely," Jim said, "you should put it on. Nice work, Cole, good choices for everyone."

As Jerica held the necklace dangling from her right forefinger, Cole moved toward her and offered to help fasten it in place. As he did, his fingers touched the back of her neck where she'd lifted her hair.

When it was nearly ten o'clock, Mary yawned and said that it just might be a good time to go home. Jim stood, pulled her to her feet, and offered his arm. "Let me have the honor of driving her ladyship home," he said with a smile.

Mary looked at Jerica. "I don't know. Would it be terrible for me to leave you here on your own?"

Cole looked up at his mother. "What am I, wallpaper? She wouldn't be 'on her own'. Jerica, you can stay for a while, can't you?" he said more as a statement than a question.

Mary laughed as Cole gave his mother a hug, then Jerica stood, embracing first Mary then Jim. "I'll be fine," she said. "Thank you both for wonderful gifts, and for making me a part of this. It really has been one of my happiest Christmases."

When Mary and Jim had bundled up against the cold and left for their homes, Cole asked Jerica if she'd like another wine or a hot drink. She opted for neither, just more sitting by the fire in the soft glow of the tree's lights and flickering candles. She sat down where Mary had been, at one end of the sofa facing the hearth. Cole sat across from her in his roomy chair, sipping the last of his brandy.

"This has been a wonderful day," Jerica said staring into the embers falling from the burning logs.

"I agree," Cole said. "I was kind of worried that you'd be stressed because of not being with your family. Being with us, I'm glad it was right for you. It was certainly right for Mom and me. She gets sad sometimes at the holidays thinking about Dad. You're good company for her, Jerica, I'm really glad you're here."

Jerica smiled at him, her eyes reflecting the soft glow in the room. "Are you only glad that I'm here for your mother's sake?" she asked teasingly.

Cole looked at her with one lifted eyebrow. She was, it appeared, flirting with him, which was perfectly okay. "What else?" he asked, and then he moved to pick up the throw she'd given him. With it opened as wide as it would stretch, he walked to the sofa, sat down beside her, and covered them both. "There," he said, "now this is the way to close a magnificent Christmas Day."

At first Jerica felt slightly panicked, but then it felt completely normal. Her left arm was against his right arm, the warmth was incredibly delicious. Murphy moved to Cole's chair and they laughed. "I'll bet he's there every time I leave the house," Cole said. Jerica smiled and was certain she could feel Cole edge closer.

Cole allowed his head to rest back against the sofa. "This is the life," he said with his eyes closed. "This throw you chose for me is nice and warm, thank you again."

Jerica smiled and thought about shifting an inch or two toward the arm of the sofa. "Guess I should have bought two," she said.

Cole raised his head and stared at her indignantly. "What? But I thought this was all part of my Christmas present."

Jerica returned the look. "And what exactly do you mean by that, Mr. McGinnis?"

"Well," he said with a tell-tale twinkle in his eyes, "I thought it was understood, one blanket, two people, we'd be sharing."

Jerica laughed. "Remind me never to give you a set of sheets."

"Really? Never?" he teased.

At that point, Jerica tossed the blanket aside and stood up. "I need a nice cold drink. Mind if I get a soda, and would you care for one?"

"No, thanks, I think I'll finish my brandy, it makes me feel all warm inside."

Jerica smiled as she walked toward the kitchen. All warm inside indeed, she thought.

When she returned to the living room she sat down in a chair opposite him.

"Oh-oh," he said. "I've scared you away."

"Not at all," she denied, "but I should probably think about going home. It's after eleven; you must be tired."

Cole sat forward and folded the blanket carelessly back onto the sofa. "I'm not tired at all. In fact, I was thinking that since you favor my kitchen so much, maybe you'd like to sit out there for a bit, enjoy my beautiful little tree on the counter, and listen to some Christmas music to properly put the day away."

Jerica smiled as she swallowed some of her drink. "I would love that."

Cole stood and extended a hand to her, pulling her to her feet. "Come on, let's sit out in our rockers where we can be sweet old folks."

Jerica laughed. "But there's only one rocker."

"That's what you think," he said as he moved toward a side pantry. From there, he pulled another old rocking chair, its seat covered in a burgundy and tan pattern.

"Oh, this is beautiful," Jerica said as she felt the cloth seat. "Where did you get this?"

"I happened to see it when I was going by a yard sale, in fact it was the day I saw you down at the docks. Remember? I'd gone down there to the hardware store. On the way home, there it was. It needed a new seat, but that wasn't a problem, I tackled it today when I got back here from our breakfast."

"It's wonderful," Jerica said. "I like the material too."

"The material actually came with it. The woman who sold me the chair, for ten dollars by the way, offered me the material. She'd always intended to cover the seat, never got around to it. All it took was some cutting and a few staples. Voila."

They stood and stared at the dark mahogany chair for a few moments, then Cole lifted it into the kitchen next to Jerica's. "Now," he said, "we each have a place to sit and rock."

Jerica sat down in her chair. "I've felt selfish, depriving you of this chair. I think I feel better now."

Cole laughed. "Can I offer you anything else? Coffee? More dessert?"

"Only if you want me to explode," Jerica said with a smile. "This soda is just what I need at the moment."

"How about some music then?" Cole asked as he moved to turn the radio on. He returned to his chair and leaned back, listening to the soft carols. They were quiet, content, until the old song, Let it Snow came on. After a few moments, Cole stood and, without a word, invited Jerica to dance in his kitchen. His right hand felt warm against the small of her back, his left hand held her right hand firmly. With each beat of the music, Jerica could feel him getting closer until his head was near to her shoulder, his lips close to her neck. She moved her head slightly to the right, accommodating the mouth that claimed the soft flesh near her throat. Within moments, their lips were together, both of his large hands pressing her back to him, both of her arms around his neck. Their journey took them to a place against the doorway into the dining room, and then to leaning toward the living room sofa, and then to the dark, polished stairway leading to his upstairs. He reached down, placing his right arm beneath the backs of her knees and carried her up to his room. Jerica felt as if she was part of a dream. She was not resistant, which wasn't her normal behavior, wanting this and whatever followed.

Cole stopped to look at her as she lay across his bed. "You can tell me no," he said, "We can go back down to the kitchen and pretend this never happened."

"It is happening," she said, and then she reached out her arms to him, their clothes discreetly discarded, their bodies one. During their night, he woke her once with his desire. A few hours later, she woke him with hers.

At just before five in the dark of morning, Jerica woke and dressed, then tiptoed out of the house. Mary, in accepting a ride home with Jim, had left the car for Jerica. Inside Mary's kitchen, she hurried upstairs to her room and bathroom where she showered, changed into jeans and a jersey, then went back down to the kitchen where she made coffee. At seven, Mary walked into the room and found Jerica reading the morning paper.

"Oh, good morning, Dear. You got home late, huh? I went to bed around midnight and you still weren't home."

"Yes," Jerica said as she poured coffee into a mug for Mary. "I did get home late."

Mary tried not to let Jerica see the smile on her lips. She guessed this handsome young couple had enjoyed a very Merry Christmas.

Chapter Seventeen

On that day after Christmas, after Cole, Jerica found herself feeling elated yet confused. Where was this going? Nothing had ever felt so right, but still there was Dan. She needed to confront her feelings for him. He'd been a part of her life for the past four years, but never with the intense feelings that she thought should be present when being in love. Those feelings were loud and clear with Cole. She loved him deeply.

"What do you have planned for today?" Mary asked as the two women tidied the kitchen after a breakfast of fruit and toast.

"I haven't really thought about it," Jerica said, realizing that all her thoughts had been of Cole. "Did you have something you'd like me to do?"

"Oh, no, Dear. I just wondered. It's such a funny day, all the excitement of the holiday has simmered down - it's anticlimactic."

Jerica thought about her night with Cole.

"Would you like to go for lunch? It's cold and snow covered outside, but we could go someplace and have a nice bowl of chowder or a sandwich. We could give Cole a call and see what he's up to; he might enjoy an hour or two out of the house away from his studies."

"I like that idea," Jerica said. She left the calling to Mary while she went back upstairs to tidy her room and to decide what would look best with her new shell necklace from Cole. She would wear that today, and perhaps every day.

At eleven-twenty, when he walked into Mary's kitchen wearing his gray parka and black gloves, there were bits of snow crystals in his hair and his eyes looked bright from the snow's glare and the cold. Jerica wanted to walk into his arms and stay there, but Mary was there too. Cole's eyes went directly to Jerica and the trace of a smile was on his lips as he said hi to her.

"Hi," she half whispered back.

Mary looked from one to the other. She loved these two young people, but she worried about how their relationship might develop. Always being Cole's mother first, she couldn't help but feel concerned for the future. "You're looking vibrant this morning, Honey," she said to Cole. "Christmas at your home was lovely, thank you again. Are we ready to cast off for lunch?"

Cole helped his mother into her coat and gave her a hug. "I think so. How would you two feel about going to Charlie's? They have great chowder if that's what you're thinking of having."

Mary looked at Jerica. "If it's okay with Jerica, it's fine with me. They have a nice sandwich menu too."

"Sounds good," Jerica said as she slipped into her coat and pulled gloves onto her hands.

The day never found Jerica and Cole alone, although they both longed for that. At two in the afternoon, Cole left his lunch companions to go home and back to his studies. He thought about how nice it would be to just have Jerica in the house, sitting and reading, or watching TV with Murphy and the traitorous cats. He smiled as he drove out of his mother's driveway. There would be other times.

While she watched him leave, Jerica had a feeling of loss and regret. She would have loved nothing more than to go with him, to share the space in which he lived. When his car was out of sight, she went upstairs and phoned her sister, Sharyn, to inquire about their Christmas. They talked for nearly an hour, about family and the probable move to North Carolina in the spring. Lying across her bed after the conversation was ended, Jerica felt more displaced than ever. She wasn't sure about what, if anything, would happen with Cole, although she hoped for everything. Had their one night encounter ruined everything? She hadn't been reckless with passion even back in high school or college. Many a boy had tried to talk her into the backseat of his car and went home disappointed. No, she thought, she had reached the age of twenty-four before making a complete mess of things. Jerica knew she needed to be honest with Dan, and that wouldn't be easy. And then there was her career, which she disliked more each day. She turned over onto her stomach and drifted off into a light sleep.

Every time the phone rang over the next few days, Jerica hoped it would be Cole, but on one occasion, it was Dan. "Hey, Sweetheart," he began, "how are you? How was Christmas? Santa good to you? I missed you so much. We were out on the slopes a good part of the day, it was fantastic."

"Oh," Jerica said, "I'm glad you're having fun. Christmas here was very nice." She wanted to say that it was spectacular, but that kind of enthusiasm was not appropriate at this time. "We had a nice dinner, it was quiet, but I kind of like it that way."

Dan laughed. "Well, we're going to have to work on your skiing abilities. I hope that by next year, we're married and then you'll be out here in Utah with us."

Jerica shuddered. That was the last place she'd want to be, for many reasons.

Two days later, while Jerica was back at work, Mary saw a car pull into her driveway. She watched as the man got out of his car and approached her front door. She met him there and realized that it was Dan.

"Hello," he said with a big smile. "I hope I'm not interrupting your day too much; I suppose Jerica's at work."

"Yes," Mary said, "she is."

"I thought that might be the case," he said, "I wanted to surprise her, so I couldn't check with her about her work schedule. I'd like to come back when she'll be here. Would that be all right with you?"

"It's all right with me," Mary said. "I don't know what Jerica had planned though, sometimes she stops on her way home for things or even for gas. She's usually home by five."

"Great. I'll be back later then. Thank you, Mrs. McGillis."

Mary decided to say nothing of his calling her by the wrong last name and did not even say goodbye. She had no use for this fellow who allowed Jerica to travel alone late at night from Hartford to Mystic. She watched him climb into his luxury car and speed away.

Cole had been thinking of Jerica constantly. Christmas night with her had been more than he'd ever imagined feeling for a woman and he wanted to be very careful not to frighten her away. He thought about what his next step should be and decided that he would spontaneously show up at his mother's around dinnertime and whisk Jerica out for the evening. He let Murphy out for a few minutes, changed into a clean set of clothes, and fed everyone just before he left for his mother's. With hope in his heart and an abundance of joy in his heart, he drove to his mother's house, started to pull in the driveway, then noticed Dan's car. With his foot on the brakes, he stared at the lights in the familiar windows, and then he again looked at that car. For a moment, he leaned his forehead against the steering wheel, then he sat up straight and drove away thinking that he should have known it was all too good to be true.

Moments later, Jerica arrived home and was surprised to see Dan's car. "What are you doing here?" she asked in the form of a greeting to him inside Mary's living room where he stiffly sat.

"Sweetheart," he said as he stood to quickly move toward her, "I've missed you so much, I decided to come back early so that we could spend New Year's Eve together. You look fantastic," he hugged her, "I'm so glad to have you back in my arms where you belong."

Jerica pulled away a bit. "You came back a week early because of New Year's Eve?"

Dan laughed. "Oh, I know you don't care about New Year's celebrations, you think people behave like fools and drink too much. I know how you feel, Sweetheart, but we'll have fun, you'll see."

Jerica hung her coat in the front hall closet and then sat down in a chair by the darkened hearth. "I'm sorry you cut your vacation short, Dan. Honestly, I'd have been fine on my own for New Year's. What is it that you have planned?"

"Well," he began as he sat down on the sofa opposite her, "I thought we'd begin with dinner at my place, because reservations at this point are impossible, and then we'd go to a party that friends of mine are hosting. After that, well, maybe we'll go back to my place to put the proper cap on the best evening of all time."

Jerica thought that the best evening had definitely been the one with Cole.

"I can't," she said.

Dan looked stunned. "Why? What's going on that you can't? Have you made other plans? You can cancel them."

Jerica stood and walked to the fireplace mantle, then turned around to face him. "I need to talk to you, Dan. We need to sort things out."

Dan stood and walked toward her, a frown on his face. "What are we sorting out, Jerica? I don't understand. I've come all the way back here to be with you and you're acting very strange. What's going on?"

Jerica stood motionless for a few moments then moved to sit down again in her chair.

"What is it?" he asked again. "What's happening? Are you mad at me for going away with my family? I'm back, Jerica. I came back just to be with you, doesn't that prove to you how much I love you?"

Jerica covered her eyes for a moment then moved her hands to her lap. "I appreciate that you thought to do this, Dan. It was very nice of you to cut everything short in Utah, but…"

"What, Jerica? What's going on?"

"Look," she said as she stood, "let's go out for coffee or something. We can talk, we owe one another that. It's been a very emotional time with my parents in Hawaii and all. Let's go out. I'm not comfortable having this conversation in Mary's house."

"Good," he said, "I don't want you to be comfortable in Mary's house. Let's go."

Jerica fetched her coat from the closet, told Mary she was going out for awhile with Dan, and then they left.

At a coffee shop near the center of town, they stopped and decided that a drive-thru would be their best option for a private conversation. After careful comments from Jerica and pointed questions from Dan, they decided to allow things to calm down for a while. "What about New Year's Eve?" Dan asked.

"Sure," Jerica said. She'd heard nothing from Cole, which she found distressing.

"So you'll come into Hartford that night and stay over?"

Jerica took a sip from the paper container filled with hot coffee. "I'll go to Hartford, but I don't want you to plan on me staying over. I want us to take things easy, Dan. I'm not sure about anything these days. I feel like I have no stability in my life, even my job is driving me to distraction. I don't want to be committed to anything. I can't manage that at this point. I want to be completely honest with you. I don't know how I feel about us. You're a good man and we've been good friends, but other than that, I don't know about a future with you. I'm sorry, I don't want to hurt you, it's just that I need some time to figure things out."

Dan looked as though he might cry. "I'll give you as much time as you need, Sweetheart. Thank you for saying you'll come to Hartford on New Year's. It gives me hope."

Jerica smiled and touched his arm, but in her heart she knew that with or without Cole, Dan could never be the one for her. She would let him down easy, the only way that he would understand how unmatched they truly were. When they said goodnight at near eleven, he reached over to kiss her before she stepped out of the car at Mary's. Jerica moved her face to receive his kiss on her cheek, and then she was gone.

Cole sat on his sofa, his feet up and crossed at the ankles on the ottoman, the blue throw from Jerica next to him. He glanced at it as he listened to the news, unable to enjoy its warmth. He'd spent the greater part of the evening reading and then correcting papers from his students. Now he had time to think and he couldn't help but wonder what had happened. How could Jerica be with him all of Christmas night then go right back into the arms of that guy. Cole stood, walked to the kitchen door and called to Murphy. He walked outside without a jacket and waited for the gentle retriever to come back into the house. He closed and locked the door, unplugged the tiny Christmas tree on his counter, leaving the kitchen in darkness, and then he went back into the living room and sat down. Cole thought about having a hot cup of coffee, but he didn't want it. He thought about pouring himself a brandy, but he didn't want that either. He put his head back on the sofa and with tormented thoughts of Jerica in Dan's arms, he fell asleep.

Chapter Eighteen

Over the next couple of days, Jerica and Cole did not meet or speak on the phone, each of them feeling miserable with missing one another. Cole made an effort to talk with his mother every day, but there was a noticeable inclination not to mention Jerica. Mary knew why, she didn't need to inquire, and she could see that Jerica, too, was in stress. She wanted to ask what had happened but it was, after all, not her place.

The day before New Year's Eve, Cole called and asked his mother what she was doing to celebrate.

"Jim's asked me to join him at the yacht club. There's a dinner, maybe some music, I'm not sure. He promised it would be an early evening; Deena's been invited as well, so it will be nice. What about you, Honey? What are you doing?"

"I'm not sure. I'll probably stay here and read. I have a lot of material to get through for my classes."

"On New Year's?" Mary questioned. "You need to go and have some fun somewhere." And then she was sorry to have added, "Jerica's going to Hartford."

Cole closed his eyes for a moment then reached down to pat Murphy's head.

"I'll see," he said. "Maybe I'll do something."

When their conversation had ended, Cole felt both in pain and angry at his own vulnerability. No one had ever made him feel so deeply until Jerica. He needed to move on; this was an interest in a girl who was unavailable. All that evening he tried to study or read for pleasure but found himself reading the same passages over and over, not comprehending anything his eyes found. Finally he decided to make a call.

"Kathy, it's Cole. How are you?"

"Cole! Hey, I've been thinking about you. I'm fine, how are you? How was Christmas?"

Cole was silent for a moment. Christmas. "It was good," he said. "How about yours?"

"Lonely," Kathy groaned. "Times like the holidays, that's when I miss seeing everyone. I couldn't take the time off to fly back up there, so I had dinner with a friend from work and that was it. I didn't even bother to put up a tree."

"That's too bad," Cole said. "So, big plans for New Year's?"

Kathy laughed. "I hate to admit how pathetic my life is, but no, no plans. Not unless you're calling to tell me you're coming down."

Cole laughed. "I seriously doubt I could even get a flight at this late date."

"Do you mean you'd come if you could? Oh, Cole. Please try. That would be so wonderful. You have no idea what that would mean to me. Please, please try."

Cole thought about it and then said, "Maybe I will. I'll give the airlines a call and see what's available. What can we do about going out in Atlanta? Won't every place be packed?"

"I don't know and I don't care. If you're here, we'll have a party together. Just try, please."

When he'd finished his conversation with Kathy, he felt almost sick thinking about Jerica. All the more reason to go, he thought. Time to get that girl out of his system. He made a call to the airlines and discovered that it was easier than he'd thought to get a flight directly out of Green Airport in nearby Rhode Island to Atlanta. He would be there in the morning. Feeling suddenly excited about the prospect of getting away, he called his mother and asked if she'd watch Murphy and the cats for a couple of days. She told him that she'd be happy to do that, but she wondered, was this nothing more than a hasty rebound interest in the wrong woman?

The flight was smooth, and while Cole tried, sleep evaded him. He wished he'd thought to bring a book. When six in the morning found him in Atlanta, he made his way by taxi to Kathy's condo. He thought it was way too early to knock on her door, so he stopped in the lobby where a coffee shop was open with offerings of Danish pastry and huge chocolate chip cookies. He opted for a cheese Danish and black coffee, which he sat and consumed at a small round table. The food felt an awful lot as if it had lodged in his throat. What was he doing here in this mild weather place so far away from home? Kathy, it was time to give Kathy a chance.

At eight-fifteen, he decided it should be okay to go up to her condo. He rang the buzzer with her name, K. Bezanson, and when the glass door to the entrance opened, he walked through and to the elevators.

"You are a sight for sore eyes," Kathy said with a lilt in her voice. "I'm so happy to see you," she said as her arms went around his neck easily.

"It's pretty nice to see you too," he said as they gave one another a light kiss on the lips.

"Come on in," she invited. "I have coffee all made, and I can make you breakfast. What would you like? This is southern hospitality you know."

Cole smiled as he placed his overnight bag down on a chair. "I'm all set; I actually had a coffee and Danish in your lobby."

"What? You ate down there? That was silly, I could have made just about anything here. Well, eggs anyway." She walked close to him and gave him a hug. "Come and sit down," she said as their bodies moved apart, "I want to look at you."

Cole laughed. "Look away. You're looking very well - I like that red thing you have on."

Kathy smiled and looked down. "Yeah, well, it was a gift from my mother. It's a fleece robe. I think she forgets that the climate down here is warm. Anyway, I'm going to go and change, you make yourself comfy."

Cole nodded then walked over to a picture window with a great view of the city. On most occasions this would be a fun trip, seeing a new and vibrant place, but he was running away and that left him with the feeling that he was simply trying to avoid pain. Maybe this hadn't been fair to Kathy, maybe he'd led her on. He decided to have a good time, but to be careful.

New Year's Eve for Jerica was not a time to rejoice: the crazy hats and horns were annoying and her life felt in turmoil. She wore a pale blue spaghetti strap knee-length dress with silver heels when she would have preferred flannel pajamas and popcorn by a fire with someone she loved. This, she decided, was the last time she would compromise her position with Dan. He had his ideas for a happy life, and perhaps they weren't wrong for him, but they weren't right for her. Next year, things would be different. When midnight came and went, Jerica told Dan she wanted to go home.

"I'm all for that," he said, thinking that she meant to his place. "Come on, let's grab our coats and get out of here."

Back at the door to his apartment building, Jerica hesitated. "No, Dan, I'm not going upstairs with you. I'm going home."

Dan looked stunned. "Jerica, it's after one in the morning. Don't tell me you're driving all the way back to Mystic tonight. That's just plain crazy."

Jerica looked down at her shoes then up into Dan's eyes. "I'm sorry if you're disappointed, I really am. I'm not a party-goer, you know that, and staying here would complicate things."

"How so?" he asked.

"I've told you, Dan, I'm figuring things out as I go. I value our relationship, but I don't think we have the same ideas about important things. I believe that we need some time and space away from one another."

Dan shook his head in disbelief. "I can't believe you're doing this," he said to her. "What am I missing here?"

Jerica looked off to the street where cars filtered by slowly. "I don't think you're missing anything, Dan. I think we're just two very different people."

"So, you're saying goodbye? Is that it?"

She looked into his eyes filled with hurt. "No, not at all. We've had some wonderful times together and I hope we can remain friends.

Although I suppose that's not going to work when one of us is linked to someone else. It's no one's fault," she said, "we're just different."

Mary thought she heard Jerica coming into the house sometime around three in the morning. She listened for the soft footsteps going upstairs, and then she turned over and went back to sleep. In the morning, she climbed out of bed early, made coffee, then drove to Cole's house to take care of Murphy and the three cats. She looked at the tiny Christmas tree, discarded by the trash container in the kitchen and felt sad for the two young people she so loved. Something had not worked the way they'd hoped, and that had been Mary's great fear all along.

Back at her own home, Mary found Jerica in the kitchen sipping coffee and eating a slice of toast.

"I was surprised to hear you coming in last night," Mary said. "I hate to think of you driving back here alone so late. How was your evening?"

Jerica placed her coffee mug down on the table. "It was the typical party, I guess. Loud horns, loud music, loud people. I don't get it. Anyway, I'd had enough of all that and wanted to come back."

Mary nodded and wondered how Cole's evening had gone.

"How about your evening with Jim? Was it nice?"

"Yes," Mary said as she sat across from Jerica. "Deena had joined us, and then we ran into another woman I used to teach with and her husband, so we sat together and it was all very pleasant. Nothing outrageous. I was more than ready for my bed at one in the morning."

"Did Cole join you for the evening?" Jerica dared to inquire.

"No," Mary said. "He wasn't sure what he would do, so he decided to go away for a couple of days."

"Oh," Jerica said with surprise in her voice. "Did he go back up to Boston?"

"No," Mary said with a bit of hesitation, "he opted for warmer weather, he went to Georgia."

Georgia. To Jerica, that meant only one thing, he'd gone to connect with that woman from Atlanta, the one who'd been at his house when she called needing his help with the lights. Her heart sank. Everything looked different to her now, all her thoughts for getting home, being back near to where he was, and he was gone. This was almost unbearable.

"Do you have plans for today, Dear? Jim invited me to dinner around two. He invited you and Cole if you were going to be around. Would you care to join us?"

Jerica stood and took her coffee mug to the sink where she ran cold water into it, and then she turned to face Mary with a forced smile. "Thank you, that's a very thoughtful invitation, but I'm absolutely ready for nothingness. I think I'd like to have a sandwich later and sink myself into a good book. Does that sound terribly unsociable of me?"

"Not at all," Mary said, and she understood completely.

"Are you taking care of Cole's pets?" Jerica asked.

"Yes, I am. They're all fine. I'll stop over there with Jim later, and then tonight, I may stay there. I know Murphy gets anxious when left alone. I'll see."

Jerica couldn't offer to go and help - it would be complete torture to be in that wonderful house with things as they were now. Everything was going absolutely haywire.

On January second, Cole arrived back in Mystic. Jerica wasn't sure if she felt a sense of relief or if it was actually worse having him close but not with her. What had happened? This wasn't the kind of man who involved himself with someone and then ignored them. It was all a mess. Jerica went back to work and performed her job as efficiently as possible, it seemed important, now more than ever, to immerse herself in her work.

On the tenth, Jerica's mother telephoned to say that they were back and that they'd welcome a visit from their eldest daughter. "Come on home," her mother pleaded. "I'm so anxious to see you, and we have a lot to talk about. Will you come?"

"Yes," Jerica said, "I will."

Two days later, on Saturday morning, Jerica flew to Ohio and was met by her father and brother. They chatted about everything and hinted that there was some big news. Jerica wondered if Sharyn had told them about North Carolina, but she didn't want them to know that her sister had confided in her first.

At dinner everyone looked at Jerica and then her mother said, "We have something to tell you. We hope you won't be upset by this, we think it's going to be a big adventure."

Jerica looked from one dear face to the other. "Okay, someone tell me what's going on."

"All right," her father said, "fair enough. Your sister informed us that they're making a move to North Carolina in the early spring." He looked for Jerica's reaction which was a smile toward her sister. "The big deal about all of this is we're going too."

Jerica wasn't sure she'd heard right. "Wait, Sharyn's moving to North Carolina and you're going too? For the trip? Not for good."

Jerica's family looked from one to the other, not sure that Jerica was happy with their plans.

"Yes, Dear," her mother said. "We're all going, even Brandon. The living there is more economically friendly, and honestly, we can't bear the thought of being away from Emily as she grows up."

Jerica shook her head. "Wow, this is such a surprise." She wondered what happened to all those times they'd spoken of returning to Connecticut, but she wasn't going to bring that up now.

"Come with us," Sharyn said with a big smile. "You hate your job anyway, you'd find something else down there, I'm sure. Come on, Jer, make the family complete; move with us."

"What about college, Brandon?" she asked. "Where will you go to school?"

"I've applied to three colleges for next year. I've been accepted to all of them, so I need to make a choice. I'm excited about it."

"I thought you had a girlfriend up here," Jerica said. "Is that over?"

Everyone laughed. "No," Brandon answered, "she's transferring down to North Carolina too. Isn't that cool?"

Jerica smiled. Was absolutely everyone and everything moving on or away from her? "I'll have to give this some thought," she said.

When she returned to Mystic, Jerica felt more confused and abandoned than ever. She didn't have any idea what she wanted to do within her career or her personal life. The thought of leaving this place that she so loved, where there were people she loved, brought tears to her eyes and a heaviness to her heart. Nothing could ever be that good again, she thought as she recalled the wonderful times with Mary and Cole, and most especially Christmas night.

Days drifted into weeks. Valentine's Day came and went without a word from Dan, which pleased her, without a word from Cole, which pained her. By early spring, Jerica's family made their move and were exuberant about their new surroundings. They'd assured her that their home, with four large bedrooms, was waiting for her to join them.

"You'd love it here, Jerica. The flowers are in bloom and the trees, there are so many different kinds. It's wonderful, and the folks here are so friendly," her mother told her on the phone. "Please give it some serious thought, Dear; we'd love having you back. It's been nearly six years since you graduated from high school and went off to college and your career. We want you back."

In early May, Jerica gave her notice at the hospital, telling them that she would be leaving in two weeks. When she told Mary that evening, it couldn't have been worse had someone taken a sledge-hammer to Mary's entire body; she couldn't believe that they were losing Jerica again. Cole had said little, but she knew he'd be devastated and she called him. It was time for these two to talk if nothing else.

Cole reacted as if he'd been given an electric shock. When he had time to calm down, he wondered what he could possibly say or do to change her mind. He expected that she was probably making the move with Dan, that there were marriage plans in the works. He pulled on a light jacket and locked the door to his house before leaving for his mother's and an overdue confrontation with Jerica. As he pulled into the driveway, he met her getting into her car.

"Hey," he said before she closed the door, "where are you off to?"

Jerica looked up at him and wanted to cry at being so near to him and yet so emotionally apart. "To the store for a couple of things," she said.

"Can we talk for a little while?"

"About what?" she asked, not sure that she could stand to be alone with him.

"I heard the news that you're planning to leave. I need to know why."

Jerica looked away through her windshield. "What does it matter?" she asked.

"We need to understand," he said. "I need to understand. Please, give me a little time here."

"Okay," she said, "let's just take my car. Is down by the water all right with you?"

"Yeah, that's fine," he said as he slid into the passenger's seat.

They drove the few miles in complete silence, Cole stealing looks at her beautiful profile. He'd questioned himself at least a hundred times: what had gone so wrong after months of playful flirting and a night that had been so right. They pulled into a space near to the seaport's museum and Jerica turned off the engine.

At first they were both quiet and then Cole spoke. "How did this happen to us?" he asked.

Jerica looked directly at him. "What is it that you're referring to exactly?"

Cole tried to stretch his legs out in front of him, but Jerica's car was small and he wished they'd brought his instead. "I wish I could put it into the right words. We had something, Jerica. I can't fathom what happened. Did I rush you? Did I not call you when I should have after? I was trying to give you space. I don't get what in hell happened."

Jerica turned away. The sun was setting and the water was becoming a very dark blue. "Everything's just been upside down," she said. "I'm not looking for someone to blame for anything that's going on."

"Why are you leaving?" Cole asked.

Jerica fought back tears. "It's time to move on, that's all. The job at the hospital isn't what I want. I've been looking into going back to school and I've decided that's the best next step for me."

"What kind of school? Where are you going?"

Jerica moved a strand of hair back from the side of her face. "I've decided that what I want to do is become a nurse. I have the basics from college, so I should be able to complete the nursing program in two years or less."

Cole thought that Jerica would make a terrific nurse, but he didn't want her to go away. "I think that's a great idea; how did you come to that decision?"

"When I went into the hospital for a few hours at Christmas, I met this nice old man. I told him about my issues with work and he suggested I might be a good nurse. I'd thought of it when I was young, in my teens, but somehow I managed to make the wrong decision and head into business rather than the humanities. I like the prospect of being able to work nights too, instead of days."

Cole nodded. "You know, there are local colleges and schools of nursing. You don't have to leave."

Jerica closed her eyes for just a moment and then looked at him. "Yes, I believe I do. Besides, I'm making the move to North Carolina. I'll live with my parents, they're only about eight miles from the nursing school I'll attend. I'll be able to pay my own way with my savings, and," she hesitated, "it will just be better all around. I need the change."

"What about Dan?" Cole asked. "Is he going too?"

Dan had been out of the picture since letting him down on New Year's. "No, Dan will stay here in Connecticut."

Cole wasn't sure that he had the right to ask any more of her. "So, you're going to school in North Carolina for two years. Then what?"

"Holy smoke, Cole, you really expect me to have figured everything out. I have so many things to take care of between now and then."

"I thought you loved it here in Mystic. Have you considered coming back here when you're through with school? Maybe you could get a job at St. Joseph's again."

Jerica nodded. "I spoke with Sally Hahn, the director of nursing here at St. Joe's. She said the same thing - they'd love to have me back as a nurse, and yes, that's a possibility. I'll see."

"When you were heading out this evening, had you eaten dinner? I was wondering if you'd like to have a bite to eat someplace. The Blue Schooner Café is just around the corner. What do you think?"

Jerica thought that anything she ate would block her throat and literally kill her. She wanted to be with him, to hear him say he loved her, but he had not done that. "Thank you," she said more stiffly than she felt, "I think I'll just pick up my things and get back to your mother's."

Cole looked at her briefly, then opened the car's door.

"What are you doing?" she asked.

"I'll stay down here for awhile," he said.

"But it's a long walk home from here; your car's at your mother's house."

Cole had a sad smile on his handsome face. "It's not that far. I'll grab a sandwich someplace and then I'll take the walk back. It's a nice evening."

"Will I see you again before I go?" she asked trying to hide the tremor in her voice.

"I don't think so," he said, and then he was gone.

Chapter Nineteen

Jerica felt like her heart had shattered. When Cole walked away from her car, within the next few seconds she imagined all sorts of things. She could see him with the woman in Atlanta, although Mary had not mentioned her. She could also visualize him working on his home, and in her arms. She wished she had dared to simply tell him the truth and accept whatever his reaction might be. After all, she thought, what did she have to lose? She dabbed at her tear-filled eyes, shifted the car into reverse and then forward. She needed a few things before her trip to North Carolina in just a few days.

When she walked into Mary's kitchen around eight that evening, Mary was having a cup of tea while she sorted through a drawer filled with odds and ends.

"Hello, Dear," she said. "I was starting to get worried about you, I didn't think you'd be gone this long. Now I sound like your mother, don't I?"

Jerica smiled and sat down at the kitchen table with her small bag. "I don't mind your motherly comments at all, Mary, I'm really going to miss you."

Mary stopped shuffling around in the drawer. "What a mess this is," she said, "I throw everything in here: old elastic bands, paper clips, pens that are all dried up, pennies - no wonder I can never find things. It was John who kept this drawer in shape. He liked it neat so he could locate a screwdriver or the tin of tacks when he needed them." Mary took her tea from the counter and sat down across from Jerica. "Want some tea, there's plenty in the pot?"

Jerica shook her head no. "Thank you, I really don't feel like anything just now, maybe later."

"You're not happy about this move, are you?" Mary asked looking at the young woman's somber face.

Jerica looked around the room and then directly at Mary. "I don't know what I'm doing, Mary. I feel very certain that the nursing will be my career answer; I wish it hadn't taken me so long to figure that out. As far as North Carolina goes, it's all going to be brand new to me. I haven't been there, I'm taking my sister's and my parents' word for it that I'll like it. I think I need to be with them now. Other than that, I have this vague feeling that I had a chance to make my life soar and that somehow I managed to turn everything into a wreck."

Mary was quiet for a few moments and then she asked, "Does any of this have to do with Cole?"

Jerica looked at Mary and smiled. "You're his mother; it's kind of hard to talk about."

"You can tell me, or you don't have to. Nothing is going to change how I feel about you, Jerica. I know Cole has deep feelings for you, that's what I know."

Jerica looked down at her folded hands. She wished that she was as certain of Cole's affections as was his mother. "He's a factor," she admitted. Then she added, "There are so many pieces to this puzzle. As much as I dread leaving here, it's time for me to figure things out, to give myself a rest. The one thing I want you to know is that you will always be a part of my life. I want you to be. I'll miss you, and I'll be back, if nothing more than for a visit, I promise."

"Have you told this to Cole?" Mary asked.

"No," Jerica said, "but if I don't see him before I go, I'd be happy to have you relay that message to him. You two are immensely important to me."

"Now," Mary began, "we're going to stay in touch, aren't we?"

"I'd love that," Jerica said. "We can plan to talk on the phone once in a while, how about that?"

Mary nodded her head, choked with emotion. "It won't be the same here without you, but I'm glad at least of the chance and the promise of talking with you often."

On Saturday morning in late May, Jerica packed her car with her clothing and a few personal affects. She had tears in her eyes and hurried as fast as she could so as not to see Mary before she left. Goodbyes were very long words, and not ones she managed well. On the kitchen table she left a note, Thank you for everything, Love, Jerica.

Knowing that Jerica was leaving that day, Cole put Murphy in the car and drove to his mother's at seven in the morning. When he saw that Jerica's car was gone, he brought the car to a stop in the street then kept going until he'd made a circle and was back at his own home. He sat in his driveway for several minutes, almost afraid to move, not trusting his legs to get him into the house. When Murphy nudged his right arm, Cole stroked the retriever's head and then switched off the engine and opened the car's door. Listless, drained of all positive energy, he walked into his house with Murphy at his side.

By nine-thirty, Jerica had been traveling Route 95 South for more than two hours and came to a service area where she could fill her gas tank and get herself a cup of tea and a muffin to eat on the road. When she'd parked her car, she sat, the morning's sun penetrating the windshield as if it was trying to put her in the spotlight, pushing her to do more than think. She was beyond tears. Everything before her was going to be brand new and the only thing she knew she could handle was a career in nursing. It was in some ways exhilarating to at least feel good about the one thing that she was going to do. In the food area, as she waited to be served, she heard a baby cry behind her and turned to see a young couple fussing over a small bundle. Jerica watched them thinking how much she wanted that kind of togetherness for herself someday. The sweet scene left her with a deep sense of loneliness for all that she'd left behind.

Having driven for more than fourteen hours, with just a couple of stops for gas and something to eat, Jerica arrived at her parents' home in the small town of New Willows, North Carolina. It was dark, nearly ten at night, when she pulled into their circular driveway. The house was alive with welcoming lights and she could see the charm of the part-fieldstone, part-wooden house. It was not home, but inside a family who loved her was waiting and she felt the intense need to be embraced.

Cole sat in his kitchen, his eyes avoiding the old rocker. The new one, the one he'd picked up for him, he placed back in the storeroom off the pantry area. What need was there for it now? He thought about putting the other one away as well, but it had the history of his grandmother; he would leave it there. He stared into his black coffee and thought that maybe he was a fool. He wondered where Jerica was. He thought of her on the road, driving alone in unfamiliar territory. He thought of her here with him: in his arms dancing, in his arms on the sofa, in his arms in his bed. It was excruciating. He took his cup to the sink and dumped the remainder down the drain then called Murphy to go out for a long walk.

Chapter Twenty

Two weeks later, on June fourth, Mary prepared Cole's favorite meal for his birthday: meatloaf with mashed potatoes and creamed corn. Her heart was heavy as she made the cake; he hadn't specified which one he wanted, so she made a known favorite: carrot cake with creamed cheese frosting. When he called her after teaching school all day, his voice lacked enthusiasm.

"I have your dinner all ready, Honey. You come over any time you want," Mary said.

Cole closed his eyes for a moment recalling his twenty-ninth birthday one year ago - the day that Jerica walked back into his life. There was little to be happy about today. He'd not had a single day without thoughts of her and what she was doing. "I'll be over around six if that's okay, Mom."

"That's fine, Honey, and Happy Birthday."

With his favorite meal consumed to please his mother, Cole was then presented with his gifts. As usual, they were practical items he'd requested and a tin box filled with his favorite sweets: chocolate brownies. With kisses, hugs, and many good wishes, Cole left his mother's house fairly early.

"Are you studying tonight?" she asked.

"Probably later," he said, "but I'm actually heading home because Kathy said she'd call tonight around eight or eight-thirty to extend her birthday wishes."

"Oh," Mary said, "that's thoughtful of her. I didn't know you were still in touch with Kathy."

"Well," he said, "we've talked from time to time. It's hard to have a relationship at this distance, but she's planning another trip up here sometime during the summer, so we'll probably see each other then."

Mary nodded. "Well you go on home then, Honey. And again, a very Happy Birthday to you."

"Thanks, Mom, everything was terrific." He leaned forward and gave his mother another hug and then left.

Mary was washing the few dishes from their meal when the telephone rang. She thought it might have been Deena or even Jim. Instead it was Jerica.

"Hello, Mary. I've been thinking of you so much and then I realized that it's Cole's birthday. I thought I might just wish him a happy day and coming year."

"That's so sweet of you, Dear. He actually just left minutes ago, maybe you could call him at home. But how are you? Do you like it there?"

"It's beautiful, Mary. My parents live in a quaint little town in a fairly large house. The old part of the house is made from field stone, the more recent part, an addition that was added sixty years ago, is of wood. The combination is really charming."

"And what are you doing with yourself? Have you investigated a nursing school down there?"

"Yes, I'm all registered, and in fact, I've already started two necessary classes. I'm excited about this career move; it will give me a purpose in life and flexibility in working hours, which I like. Being with Mom and Dad again after several years of living on my own is, well, interesting."

Mary laughed. "Yes, I can imagine. We parents forget that we instilled strength in our children and they should be able to function on their own. But, that doesn't stop us from worrying or from giving all the free advice our children can pay for."

Jerica laughed. "Well, it's not so bad. I guess it's just that I'm used to being on my own, making my own good or not so good decisions, and that's all changed now. I do like playing checkers with my dad, and the occasional game of chess, which he wins, and I like the calm times with Mom, sipping tea and checking on the flowers in her gardens. It's all good, but I can't say I feel at home here. I miss Mystic."

"You're welcome back here, right in this house, any time you want, Jerica."

"I know that, Mary, and I'll take you up on it someday: you'll see. I think I'll try giving Cole a quick birthday call. I felt bad when I realized I'd forgotten to send a card."

"Speaking of cards," Mary said, "I have one here for you but I had no address."

"It's Nineteen Lansdowne Street, New Willows, North Carolina." Jerica replied.

"Okay," Mary said, "I'll send this card off to you tomorrow. I hadn't forgotten that your birthday was June first, Dear. I felt sad to miss the chance to give you a nice big birthday hug. Anyway, I'll let you go so that you can call Cole. I think he'd love to hear from you."

Jerica dialed Cole's number and heard a busy signal. She tried again several times up until eleven o'clock - still busy. She sat down and held the small cell phone in her hands. He obviously was speaking with someone else, and who but a woman, would be talking to him for hours? She left the phone on the table next to her bed and went into the bathroom for a shower. She tried one more time at nearly midnight, still, a busy signal. She went to bed, distraught that he was so far away from her.

The next Saturday morning, Cole called his mother to see what she was doing for the weekend. Kathy had decided to come up for a visit and he thought it best to make sure all was well with his mom before he cleared the way.

"I may actually be going to Cape Cod with Deena, Honey. Just for the one night; we'd be back tomorrow later in the day. Her sister lives there and she's invited us so many times. At last, Deena's knee is in good enough condition for us to walk around and see the sights."

"Sounds nice," Cole said. "It's been years since I was last up there, I think that summer that you, Dad, and I spent the week out on the Vineyard was the last time. That had to be, what, eleven, twelve years ago?"

"I think so," Mary said. "It's been a while. What about you, Honey? What are you doing?"

"Kathy wants to catch the Red Eye tonight; she's thinking she'll come up from Sunday to Tuesday."

"Oh," Mary said. "Is she staying with her folks?"

Cole smiled because he knew what his mother was thinking. "Yes, I do believe she's planning on staying with her parents, Mom."

"I'm not prying," Mary said, but she knew that she was. "Did you have a nice talk with Jerica?"

"Jerica? I haven't spoken with Jerica since before she left, why did you ask?"

Mary frowned to herself and wondered why the girl hadn't made the call. "She called here to wish you a happy birthday. You'd just left to go home, but she said she'd try you there."

Cole sat down in one of his kitchen chairs. He'd been on the phone all night, right up until midnight, with Kathy. Finally he said, "She may have tried, Mom. I was on the phone most of the evening."

Mary said nothing. She could easily figure out that it was Kathy on the end of the line. Although she'd never met the girl, Mary had the feeling that this was a woman who recognized what a great catch Cole McGinnis was and that wasn't what she wanted for her son. It was, however, out of her hands.

When Cole placed the phone back in place, he sat with his hands in a steeple position, his fingertips touching his lips. He needed to call Kathy back to tell her the plan was a go, but that wasn't what he wanted. He wanted Jerica. He longed for Jerica.

"Kathy," he said into the phone, "before you make the trip up here, I need to be completely honest about something."

Kathy laughed with a nervous edge to her voice. "This sounds ominous," she said. "Should I be frightened?"

Cole felt bad that he'd upset her. Because she wasn't Jerica didn't make her an unworthy companion. "I just want you to know what's what. I've got a lot going on between teaching school and going to school. I don't want to mislead you. I'm not in a position to get involved in a serious relationship, that's all. I had one of those a while back and it wasn't meant to be. The last thing I want is to get you up here on false pretenses."

"Look, Cole," Kathy said, "to begin with, yes, I like you very much, more than very much. But my family is in Mystic too. I enjoy the visit with everyone, and seeing you would absolutely be the icing on the cake. That's all."

Cole rubbed his eyes. "Okay, I hear you. So, when are you expecting to catch a flight? Would you like me to pick you up or have you made other arrangements?"

"I'd love to have you pick me up if that works for you. I should be at Green around eight in the morning. I'll treat you to breakfast."

Cole smiled. "You're on," he said, "but bring lots of money. I don't think you've seen what I eat for breakfast."

"I think I can handle it," Kathy said with an air of relief in her voice. "I'll see you in the morning."

Cole sat next to the phone for several minutes. If it weren't for his intense feelings for Jerica, Kathy would definitely be a contender for his affections. She was beautiful, smart, and willing to make concessions for him. He needed to give this a chance. Maybe in time, he'd get over Jerica.

That same Saturday morning, Jerica scuffed about in bare feet, not entirely used to the North Carolina heat in mid-June. With her parents out shopping for groceries and a new patio set, Jerica poured herself a glass of orange juice and soda water, then walked outside to the roomy front porch filled with natural hickory chairs. The yard, draped in several weeping willow trees and colorful groups of flowers, was a beautiful sight. She sat down in a rocking chair and propped her feet up on a small matching ottoman. In the distance, out on the street, she watched as an elderly man walked his tan colored dog and she thought about Murphy. She loved Murphy, and then she thought about all she'd left and loved in Mystic. As beautiful as it was in North Carolina, it wasn't home. It was a good place to be at this time in her life, and it would be a wonderful place to return to for reunions with her family, but Jerica knew she would want to go back to Mystic. There was no doubt in her mind. When she'd leisurely finished her drink, she walked back into the house to retrieve her books for nursing school. She returned to the porch and sat down, smiling as she thought of Cole studying for his Masters. The two of them were back in school.

Cole spent his first summer in years not teaching sailing. He concentrated on the work he needed to complete to get his degree as quickly as possible. With weeks off from teaching, he made two visits to Atlanta and one to Boston, where a group of former college friends had decided to gather for a weekend. Every once in a while he'd test himself about Jerica. He'd allow himself to remember being with her. Every time, the longing for her was still there, stronger than ever.

Jerica and her family, not used to the heat and humidity of the south, made it through the summer by staying inside, often with the central air conditioning. They equated staying in out of the heat with staying in out of the cold up north. By Thanksgiving, Jerica had spoken with Mary several times, but not with Cole. She missed him. She thought of him constantly. The past Thanksgiving in Mystic had been wonderful, everything she could have wished for. Now she was preparing vegetables and planning the desserts for celebrating with her family. She expected this holiday to be filled with warmth and joy; nothing could take that away, but thinking of Mary and Cole, she wished that they were a part of this too.

Chapter Twenty-One

Thanksgiving Day was not going to be the same for Mary and Cole. Each was aware of the void left by Jerica's absence. Although neither of them mentioned her name, they thought about her and what she had brought to their lives. Mary had invited Jim while Deena was going to her nephew's home as usual. Cole thought about inviting Kathy; she'd hinted that she'd love to be spending the holiday with him, but thinking about last Thanksgiving, he simply couldn't bear to extend the invitation. He felt very guilty about that. Kathy had been obviously eager to please and she deserved to own a part in someone's life. Cole had not misled her, but he hadn't pushed her away either. Maybe it was coming to that. Maybe that would be the fair thing to do. He thought about it frequently, but not as frequently as he thought about Jerica living in New Willows, North Carolina.

Mary fussed with the stuffing and prepared the usual vegetables. After she'd placed the pumpkin pies into the oven, she called Jerica. She felt the need to connect.

"How are you, Dear? We're really and truly missing you this Thanksgiving."

"Mary, you don't know how many times I wanted to call you last evening while I was making pecan pie and preparing some of the vegetables. Even with Mom and Dad bustling around with me in the kitchen, my memories of being with you and Cole were overwhelming. I miss you very much, both of you. How are Murphy and the cats? I miss them too."

Mary laughed. "My bet is that they miss you as well. They're fine. Cole still refers to the cats as traitorous. He said they were all over you every time you were there."

Jerica smiled. "I miss not having pets. Mom still won't get one, although there's a cat hanging around and I've seen her slip it some food."

"How are your sister and her family? Are they happy down there? The job working out all right for them?" Mary asked.

"They love it here. My brother-in-law has wonderful opportunities at work and their home is wonderful, much more of what they wanted than they could have had in Ohio. And my little niece is roaming all over the place. Mom spends a lot of time over there with her so that my sister can substitute teach. My mother would never want to be too far away from Emily; it's the first grandchild thing, I think."

"And your father, I'm sure he's enjoying that little one too."

Jerica smiled. "Yes, he is."

"Well," Mary said, "I suppose you'll go off on your little morning shopping spree tomorrow as usual? Pick up a few Christmas gifts?"

"Actually, I can't. I have classes in the morning and then I need to pull duty in the hospital from noon until eight at night. No day after Thanksgiving off for me this year. Mom and Sharyn will go though - they wouldn't miss it."

Mary thought she heard a sense of sadness in Jerica's voice. "Are you really happy down there, Dear? Is everything okay?"

"Yes," Jerica said, "it is. It's just different, I'm getting used to things."

"What's different? Besides the weather."

Jerica sat down and smiled. "Well, for one thing, everyone down here has a front porch. I love the porches. They're kind of a space in the middle, where you're not in the house, but you're still part of it. When people walk by, they chat, and sometimes they get invited up for lemonade. It's very friendly. I think I'd always want a porch on my house."

Mary nodded, that did sound nice. She and Cole both had patios. "I can see why you'd like the porch, it sounds very appealing."

"Who's joining you for dinner today?" Jerica asked.

"Oh, it'll be the usual suspects, Cole and Jim will be here for dinner. Jim's daughter is going to her in-laws this time, so he was happy to be invited again. I invited my sister, but she went to spend a few days with her children, which is what I'd hoped for, she's been acting very down lately. We're keeping it simple, but we still manage to enjoy the day. Of course, we'll stuff ourselves, and then, well, I suppose we'll watch White Christmas as always."

Jerica felt very sad thinking about that; she'd so loved their tradition of taking a walk and returning to watch the movie.

"Come to think of it," Mary said, "maybe we should try something else this year. I think I'll suggest to the boys that we consider seeing a movie at the theatre. There are a few good ones out just now and it would get us out of the doldrums."

Jerica wiped the tears from her eyes. "Maybe you're right," she said. "It might be fun to do something else for this year."

After their conversation, Jerica stood still for a few moments and looked out at the back yard of her parents' home. There was prettiness everywhere she looked, and yet it wasn't where she wanted to be.

After their Thanksgiving feast, Mary, Jim, and Cole took a walk toward the center of town. None of them spoke when approaching Braeden's Creek, each of them recalling that Cole had taken Jerica there one year ago at this time. They edged toward the small shops, browsing in the windows, pointing out particularly interesting objects. On their walk home, Mary suggested they might consider a movie at the theatre rather than staying at home. Cole and Jim both agreed that it might be a nice change.

"I called Jerica," Mary dared to say.

Cole looked at his mother, then he looked at the scenery before him as they walked.

"How is she?" Jim asked. "She is certainly one lovely young lady. I miss her."

"She's doing well. She's getting on with her nurse training, likes it a lot. She misses us too though, all of us," Mary said.

"Wish I could guess what's keeping her down there," Jim said. "Did she say much about it, what it's like?"

Mary smiled. "She likes the front porches."

Jim laughed and Cole felt slightly puzzled. "The porches?" Jim asked.

"Yes. She loves the friendliness of them, the hospitality one might offer to the passersby. She said that someday, she'll want a house with a front porch."

Cole walked and couldn't help but smile as he thought about how his house would look with a front porch. Not bad.

"Okay," Mary said, "dessert and a movie, or the movie and dessert?"

Chapter Twenty-Two

With Christmas just around the corner, Mary called Cole to ask if he could take the time to get her tree up and the lights positioned. She knew he was busy, but she also knew that he'd been dragging his feet through the holidays and she believed it was due to missing Jerica. Mary missed her too; the enthusiastic attitude of that young woman was contagious. With her gone, everything seemed less exciting. Maybe if Mary put some energy into getting ready for Christmas, Cole would begin to feel in a more festive mood. It was just as she had feared - her son fell in love with Jerica and the landing was proving to be painful.

Cole rubbed his brow and leaned against his kitchen counter. "No problem getting the decorations going, Mom. How about tonight? I could get the tree down from the attic and we can get the lights the way you like them. I feel bad; we're late with getting trimmings up this year. I can't believe we have less than two weeks until Christmas. I haven't bought a single gift either."

Mary polished a small oval table in the living room as she listened. "It's okay, Honey. If I'd been ready for the tree with my usual urgency, I'd have hounded you about it. As for the gifts, I need to shop too. I want to get something in the mail to Jerica, just some little thing."

Cole took a deep breath. "Yeah, I may do that too. It sure isn't like last year, is it? We were hopping around getting everything in order." He thought about adding the question, was that about Jerica? He knew it was: there was no need to ask. "After we get the tree up, would you want to go out for a burger and then hit the shops? Maybe you could help me with my gift selections."

"Oh," Mary said, "that would be fun. Yes, let's do that, I'd really love it."

"Okay. I'll drop by around three. We'll work up an appetite getting the tree organized, then we'll go out. We're due for some fun."

Mary smiled and felt tears trickle down her cheeks. She felt that when they lost Jerica, they had also lost a bit of one another, each one missing that sweet girl. Mary was thankful for getting even a small portion of her son back.

After a meal of sandwiches and coffee at a café in the village, they browsed the shops for gifts. In one store window, Cole spotted a foot high tree decorated all in tiny seashells. At its top sat a small starfish. It was perfect. "I don't know how I'll package that thing," he said to his mother, "but it looks like something Jerica would like." Inside, they discovered that the store would package and mail the little tree for them.

A bit further on, Cole and Mary looked through another window at toys where teddy bears of all sizes sat perched on a pretty sleigh. "That little bear," Cole said, "the blue one with the bright little eyes, would you like that to add to the collection Jerica started for you?"

Mary laughed. "One bear makes a collection? Actually, yes, I'd love it."

They walked into the store and, while Cole purchased the blue bear for his mother, Mary decided that fair was fair as she selected a white bear with a blue ribbon around its neck to send to Jerica. Again, the store offered to package and mail the gift to North Carolina. With their gift buying well underway, Cole and Mary stopped for a cup of hot cocoa and they were home by nine.

"How would you like to handle dinner this year, Honey?" she asked as Cole helped her out of her coat. "Would you like me to do it here? It's just the three of us; Jim's decided to join us after spending the morning at his daughter's."

Cole thought about it; he didn't even have a tree up yet. "I don't know, let me think about it, Mom." And then he said, "No, let's just keep it at my place. I need to get off my duff and put up a tree. We can do the steaks on the grill again, that was nice and easy. What do you think?"

Mary smiled and hugged him. "I think that's a great idea. I'll tell Jim."

Cole drove home and thought about Kathy. Again, she'd had hopes of spending the holidays with him, but this holiday above all was Jerica's and he couldn't invite someone else into that space. He decided to send Kathy a beautiful arrangement of Poinsettias for Christmas with pink, white, and red plants all in one decorative container. After the holidays were over, he would talk with her; it was time.

Jerica was thinking about Christmas in Mystic. The snow on the ground made it all so magical. There was no snow in New Willows; the grass was green and there were still some flowers in bloom. As she tied red ribbons on packages for her family, she was pleased that she'd found small gifts that were representative of the area for Mary and Cole, and even a container of sweetened pecans for Jim. As she folded a soft, hand made scarf into a box for Mary, she planned on the best way to send these gifts since Cole's present was a hand-blown glass sailing ship to hang at one of his windows. She would pack it with great care, tucked in and among the soft toys she'd purchased for Murphy and the cats, before taking it off to the post office.

"Look at what we found at Shelton's Toy Mart," Jerica's mother exclaimed as she walked into the kitchen where Jerica was wrapping her gifts. "Have you ever seen anything cuter? Didn't you have a doll like this one when you were little?"

Jerica stopped what she was doing and looked at the toys. "Oh, Emily is going to love that doll. Yes, I had one similar to that one. I love that pink outfit too. You and Dad had a good time shopping, didn't you?"

Jerica's mother laughed and admitted she'd gone a bit overboard.

On Christmas Eve, around nine o'clock, Jerica took advantage of having the quiet house to herself to call Mary. Her parents had gone over to Sharyn's to help amuse Emily while they put toys together for the next day.

"I'm so glad you called, Dear. I wanted to call you, but you know: I don't want to intrude on your time with your family. How are you? How's everything going with school and such?"

"It's going well. I'm keeping up with everything and I've actually taken on more courses than I need to, but the sooner I finish up, the sooner I get to begin my career. I think this is absolutely the best thing I could have done, Mary; I know I'm going to love it."

Mary smiled and sat down to talk, dusting flour from her hands. "I suppose you're doing some of your wonderful cooking. We're going to miss your French Pancakes for breakfast tomorrow."

Jerica smiled. "I can tell you how to make them; they're really easy."

"You know what?" Mary said, "It wouldn't be the same. We'll wait until you come back and make them for us. Any visits planned for up this way?"

Jerica frowned to herself. "I wish I could say yes to that, but I'm so busy between studies and work. Maybe later in the spring, or even in the summer - I'm not sure."

"Well, I don't know what the exact schedule will be at this point, but Cole's nearly through with his Masters. I've talked to Jim about giving Cole a surprise combination party: his birthday and completing his schooling. It would be wonderful if you could come up for that, but of course, that's five months away."

Jerica paced as she listened to Mary. "We'll see what happens," she said. "I'd love to be there for those occasions. I don't know how he accomplishes so much; he has the house to take care of too."

"Oh," Mary said, "wait until you see the house. He's been putting together some new things, got a little help from a friend, but he works on it himself when he has time."

"I thought he was nearly done. It's such a wonderful old house; I can't imagine that it needed much more. His love for the place really shows. You've raised quite a remarkable son, Mary."

Mary smiled. "May I pass that compliment on to him?" she teased.

Jerica laughed. "You're his mother; I'll leave that to you. How's Jim? Anything new on the horizon with him?"

"You mean with him and me, don't you?" Mary laughed. "No, we're good friends. I will admit that he's growing on me. I find that when I don't see him, I miss him, but as for taking vows, no, I haven't changed my mind. And I think this arrangement appeals to Jim now as well. After all, he's free to visit his children when he wants to, and I'm free to see Cole or one of my friends whenever I wish without checking in, and seeing one another twice a week is very comfortable. We're good. What about you, Dear? I haven't heard you mention Dan or anyone else for that matter."

"I don't have time for much other than my present life," Jerica said wistfully. "At this point, I'm happy to just be carrying on, getting my life in order so that I can look to the future with clarity." She wanted to ask about Cole, was he seeing anyone, was he still involved with the woman from Georgia, but she restrained herself and did not inquire. Instead she said, "I received the packages from you and Cole today. I'm dying to open them, but I'll wait until Christmas morning. I hope you received the package I sent; it has a little something in it for each of you, Jim included."

"That was so thoughtful of you, Dear. I have the parcel right in front of me. I think that now that you've told me there's something there for Jim, we'll just wait and open the box at Cole's tomorrow after dinner."

Jerica felt a lump in her throat. Tomorrow, Christmas, what a wonderful day, and night, it had been. "Who will be with you?" she dared to ask, hoping for the right answer.

"Just the three of us: Jim's staying with us for dinner this year. He decided to visit his daughter early in the morning, to see the children with their loot from Santa, and to have a kind of brunch with them. I'm glad he's coming, and Cole will do his magic with the steaks on the barbeque again. Wish you were going to be here too."

Jerica felt warm tears on her face. "Will you tell Jim and Cole that I wish them a wonderful Christmas? And give the cats and Murphy a pat for me? There are little gifts in the package for them as well."

Mary smiled: that was so Jerica. "I'll tell the men in my life, and I'll give those hairy little friends of yours their gifts. We're going to miss you so much, Dear."

When she placed the phone back in place, Jerica decided she couldn't wait to open the boxes from Mary and Cole. When she saw the tiny tree with its variety of shells and the starfish at the top, she cried. He was pulling her back to the sea all the more with this little tree and its ocean gems. Jerica sat and held the tree for some time, then she placed it in the center of the kitchen table with thoughts of moving it to her room later. When she opened the gift from Mary, the teddy with the blue bow, Jerica cried again. He was beautiful, so soft, such a bright-eyed little thing. She hugged the bear, then she sat it in a chair until she could move it and the tree to her room.

On Christmas morning Cole stood at his kitchen window drinking a cup of coffee as he watched Murphy navigate the snowdrifts in the backyard. It was a comical scene as the dog looked around with the question in his eyes, where did all this white stuff come from? Cole felt a sense of sadness for the Christmas prior, so much happiness in going to his mother's where Jerica prepared breakfast, and then her going to the hospital before joining them all for dinner. It had been beyond wonderful. He reminded himself that they were lucky, everyone was well, he was grateful for that, but it didn't stop him from missing her. As he opened the door to welcome Murphy back inside, the phone rang and he picked it up to hear Kathy's voice.

"Hi Handsome," she teased. "Merry Christmas. And what are you up to this morning?"

Cole smiled; she was a great girl. "At the moment, I'm having coffee and drying a sopping wet dog."

Kathy laughed. "How did he manage to get wet?"

"Well, there's snow up to his belly here; he dragged himself around in it long enough to gather a fair amount from his chest down."

"It's very pretty though; I'm enjoying it."

Cole stood up straight and threw the towel onto a chair. "You've got snow in Atlanta?"

Kathy laughed. "I have no idea what's in Atlanta: I'm in Mystic."

Cole felt stunned. He had no idea that she had plans to come up this way for the holidays.

"Hey, you there?" she asked when he made no comment.

"Yeah. Wow, you took me by surprise."

Kathy sighed. "Sweetie, I'd take you by surprise or any way I could."

Cole sat down. "So, you're here. When did you get in?"

"I walked into my parents' house about twenty minutes ago. Dad picked me up at Green. When do I get to see you?"

Cole crossed his right ankle over onto his left knee. "I don't know. What are your plans? How long are you here for?"

"I fly back tomorrow night, so just the two days. I hope you can make time to see me today."

Cole wished he'd had a talk with her before this; it wasn't fair to keep her clinging to the possibility of the two becoming one. "Of course I'll see you today. I have guests coming for dinner around three, what's your schedule like? I would suspect you're dining with your family."

"I guess so, yes. But when can I see you then? What time will your guests be going home? Maybe we can properly close the day."

"That might be kind of late," Cole said. "Last year they didn't leave until around nine or ten."

Kathy smiled and curled her legs beneath her body in her father's recliner. "That's okay," she said, "I could be at your place in ten minutes if you give me a call when they're gone. What do you think?"

Cole was thinking that he wasn't ready for this. Last Christmas with Jerica had been beyond any expectations he could have dreamed. To be fair to Kathy, he needed to divert her attention to something other than coming to his place late at night. "I'll call you later," he said, "when my guests have gone." They talked for another half hour then ended their call with wishes for a Merry Christmas and plans for later that evening.

Cole leaned forward in his chair and rested his forehead on the palms of his hands, his elbows on his knees. This was getting complicated and he'd allowed it to happen. Those trips to Atlanta had meant more to Kathy than to him and it hadn't been fair. He was using her to try getting over another woman and it just wasn't working.

After dinner with Jim and his mother, they opened their gifts. The first package they decided upon was the one from Jerica. Mary tossed catnip mice to the cats and a squeaky soft toy to Murphy. He sniffed it and then looked at Cole, as if he'd picked up the scent of an old friend and wondered where she was. Mary handed a brightly wrapped tin to Jim which was filled with cinnamon and sugar roasted pecans. For Mary there was the soft, hand-made scarf in swirling colors of lavender, tan, and cream, and for Cole, the glass sailboat. Jerica had thought of everything.

At nine-thirty Mary yawned and suggested that she and Jim should go along. "It was wonderful as always, Honey," she said to Cole. "Thank you for everything."

"You too, Mom, and Jim, Merry Christmas; it was nice to have you with us."

The three hugged goodbye and, at the same time, Cole urged Murphy outside for one last time that night. When the dog walked back into the kitchen and gave himself a good shake to rid himself of the snow, Cole laughed and wiped Murphy and the floor down with a few paper towels. He stared at the telephone for a moment; he knew what he had to do.

"Hi Kathy," he began. "My guests have gone, I wondered if you'd like to join me for a Christmas nightcap."

"I've been waiting all day for just that," she said. "I'll be right over."

"Hold on just a minute. I'll pick you up."

"Why? I can easily get over to your house. Why should you go out to pick me up?"

Cole shifted his weight from one foot to the other. "There's a new café in town I thought you'd like. We can have something there."

There was a hesitation from Kathy's end of the line. "You mean we're going out someplace? We aren't going to be at your place?"

"You'll like the Schooner; it's nice, quiet."

"All right, if that's what you want," she said in a subdued tone.

In a darkened corner of the café, where Christmas lights twinkled around the bar's large mirror, Cole sat with Kathy, allowing her to begin.

"Something's off with us, isn't it?" she said.

"It isn't so much that something's off, it's more that it's not on. And before you say anything, Kathy, let me just say that none of this is your fault, it's mine."

"I don't understand," she said as the waiter approached. "White zin for me, please," Kathy said. Cole ordered a brandy for himself.

Cole looked at Kathy's pretty face. "I don't think I fully understand it myself," he said. "Any guy I know would be tripping over their own feet to get to a girl like you. The issue is my past; I haven't managed to shake it away. I'm not ready for being committed to someone else. Between schooling, teaching, and working on my house, it gets pretty crowded in my world sometimes. Above all, it isn't because you aren't fantastic, you are."

Kathy looked away for a moment then back at him as the waiter placed their drinks before them. "I had the feeling that something was not working for us," she said. "I thought that if it was going to work at all, this was the time to give it a try. I'm head-over-heels for you, Cole, but I don't hold you responsible for how I feel. You've been pretty resistant; I knew something was holding you back."

"I'm sorry," he said.

"No, don't be. I'm not. I'm glad I had the chance with you, but to be completely honest, I met someone about a month ago and I've held him at bay until I knew what was happening with us. He's not you, but he's a nice guy and I think it's time I gave him a whirl."

Cole nodded and smiled.

Chapter Twenty-Three

With Christmas over, Jerica felt she had permission to get on with her life. Training to become a nurse was taking much of her time and energy and she was glad not to have the minutes and hours to think about all she longed for in Mystic, Connecticut. Her last few months in North Carolina had been life changing: so much to think of on every level.

After studying until nearly midnight one early January evening, she decided it was time to write thank you notes to Mary and Cole. Her note to Mary was warm and personal, while Cole's note, which took her much longer to write, was kept polite but impersonal. It took much thinking and rewriting to convince herself that she was not seeming to him to be alone or lonely, yet she was. It was impossible for her to think of spending her life with anyone but Cole; it would not be fair to the person she was with, and it would certainly not be fair to Jerica. She placed postage stamps on the two pale blue envelopes and then left them on the kitchen table where she knew that someone would take them to the post office.

"How are the studies going?" her mother asked the next morning over coffee and English muffins. "Dad took your mail off for you. Were they thank you notes for Christmas gifts?"

"Yes," Jerica said, "I've been delinquent about doing that; I just felt it was time."

Jerica's mother smiled. "You miss them, don't you?"

Jerica nodded. "I do. I miss it all, Mom. Does that upset you to hear? I love being with all of you, but Mystic is just under my skin."

Her mother reached over and patted her daughter's hand. "It doesn't upset me at all. I'll miss you when you go, but I understand that this new place was your sister's choice, and then Dad's and my choice. I just hope that you'll always come back often to visit us. I think we all know in this family that you're biding time."

Jerica smiled. "I guess I've been pretty transparent. And I don't want you to worry. I mean, I'm not expecting to go back there and fall into Cole's arms. He's probably firmly settled in with someone else by now. I'm okay with that. I know I'll still have Mary in my life, and I'll meet others as a nurse at St. Joseph's. There were lots of women my age there, just not in administration. I really didn't have the chance to meet and mingle with them. Now I will."

"I have complete faith in your future, Sweetheart. I know you love Mystic, and some of its inhabitants, and I know that with your character, you're going to be a fantastic nurse. I have no fears or hesitation about how you'll handle your future. That's a very pleasant feeling for a parent to have about their child. I wish I felt that certain about your brother and sister."

Jerica looked surprised. "What do you mean, Mom? What's going on with them, they seem fine."

Her mother smiled and said, "Well, for the most part, they are fine. I worry about your brother because he seems to have fallen in love easily and awfully young, and as for Sharyn, well, she's not as strong as you are. She needs support. Not that we all don't need it sometimes, but Sharyn, she's much more dependent on Dad and me. I don't honestly know if she'd have really moved here without us. She talked long and hard to us about coming here to live. I like it here, never got truly attached to Ohio, but honestly, I always thought we'd one day return to Connecticut. I guess we'll have to be content to visit there, to be with you and to enjoy the old haunts."

"Eventually," Jerica began, "I hope to buy a home there, and believe me, Mom, there will always be plenty of room for you and Dad to stay for as long as you wish. And I won't be a stranger to North Carolina either - it's beautiful here, I'll be back often."

167

When Jerica left for school, her mother watched her walk to the car and then drive away. They'd missed many years together, but at the same time, Jerica and she would always be bonded to one another. The distance between North Carolina and Connecticut would not part them. She walked back toward her glassed-in rear porch where tender plants were waiting to be grown outside. It was an overcast day but still pretty with all the green grass and native growth braving the mild Atlantic coast winter.

Jerica made the drive to school in minutes, collecting her thoughts about an exam she faced and a paper she had completed over the weekend. Although she was a grade A student and took to the nursing courses with ease, she always questioned herself over and over, wanting to do her best. As she pulled into a parking space and turned off her car engine, she reached for her books and her purse in the passenger's side next to her and caught sight of something red stuck in the slot at the back of the seat. She tugged at it and as she pulled it out, felt the tears spill down onto her pretty face. It was a red and white bandana from Cole's beloved dog, Murphy. She recalled the day when he'd lost it while playing in Cole's backyard. Jerica had picked it up, stuffed it into her pocket and had forgotten about it. Days later, she'd pulled it out of her pocket and left it in the car, and now, there it was as a little red flag reminder, don't forget me. She dried her tears and thought how she absolutely couldn't wait for the day when she would return to Mystic and the life she felt was meant to be. As much as she loved Mystic and all its offerings, Jerica understood quite clearly that it was Cole and Mary who held her heart.

Chapter Twenty-Four

It was on May second at eight-fifteen in the evening when Jerica received a call from Mary. "How are you, Dear? I know you're working hard on getting that nursing degree, but I hope you're managing to have some fun as well."

Jerica shifted the telephone to her shoulder in order to free her hands. "I'm doing great, Mary. It's so nice to hear your voice, is everything all right?"

"Oh, yes," Mary said, "everything's good here. I'm actually calling you in the hopes I might lure you up for a visit. I'm going to throw Cole a birthday party in combination with getting his Masters. The degree will come this month and, of course, his birthday is June fourth. He's worked so hard this past year, between school and working on his house, it's been kind of hectic."

"I thought his house complete as it was; it's such a charming old place," Jerica said.

Mary smiled. "Well, you'll be surprised then. He added something I think you'll find interesting."

Jerica wasn't sure how to ask about Cole's love life. It would be devastating to hear that he'd found someone so soon. "When is the party, Mary? I'm not sure I can get away at this point, there are tests and such."

"I'm hoping to do the party right on his day, on Sunday, June fourth. But if that day won't work for you, I'll change things. I so want you to be here," Mary said.

Jerica hesitated and shifted the phone to her other ear and shoulder. "What about Cole? Wouldn't it be awkward for him if I was there? The last thing I'd want to do is make him uncomfortable."

"No," Mary said firmly, "there is no way you'd make him uncomfortable. Jerica, he has no one in his life. That gal from Atlanta, Kathy, he talked with her at Christmas and did the honorable thing with her - he let her go."

Jerica swallowed hard, half-sad and half-happy to hear that Cole was not involved with anyone at this time. "My last classes are on May twenty-seventh," she said. "I'll call you before I leave, but I'll be there, Mary. In fact, I can't wait."

When Jerica placed the phone back on its wall receiver, she cried. It was happening sooner than she'd thought it might, but it was happening: a reunion with the man she loved. Immediately she began to think what she could give to him as a gift and as quickly as she wondered, she had her answer and it would be a wonderful surprise, she was certain.

The month seemed to rush by, laden with exams and papers and necessary tasks which now filled Jerica's busy life. On June first, her own birthday, early in the morning, she made a call to Mary to let her know that she was getting into her car to leave for the journey north. She'd be spending the first night with a friend in Virginia, and then she expected to be in Mystic by the evening of June third.

"I'm thrilled that you're coming," Mary said. "Cole is going to be so wonderfully surprised. And by the way, Dear: Happy Birthday. I haven't forgotten that magical day when your parents told us of your birth, and then they brought you home on Cole's birthday and he truly thought you were his. It was so cute, Jerica."

Jerica smiled as the tears washed down her face. She wanted to say that he was right, she was his, but instead she spoke about the trip and how much she was looking forward to seeing everyone and Mystic again. It had been just over a year since she'd left everything behind. It was exhilarating to think of going back.

On the first night of her trip, Jerica stayed with a friend from college who now lived in Virginia, just outside of Washington, D.C. It had been a long drive with a few stops to stretch her legs and to refresh with food and too many cups of coffee. But she was excited, the weather was wonderful and the scenery pleasant, even all along the highway. The next morning, she began the drive north again, planning that when she arrived on the third, she would call Mary after checking into a Mystic area hotel.

"Come and stay at the house with me," Mary invited when Jerica called. "I thought you'd just plan on that, Dear, but I should have mentioned it."

Jerica smiled. "That's okay, Mary; I really think that to keep my visit a surprise, it's best for me to stay here at the hotel. Is there something I can bring or do to help?"

"Goodness, no," Mary said. "Your coming is the grand prize. I've got a caterer doing most of the food, but, of course, I had to make the carrot cake and the brownies, so I made six carrot cakes and five dozen brownies. You know Cole: those are his favorites."

Jerica remembered well. "What time will you begin the festivities?"

"Cole is coming over at around four. I told everyone else to just come in after that, because if he saw all the cars, he'd know. This way, he'll be here, people will just begin to show up, about eighty of them. The caterers are setting things up in the dining room; I'll keep him out on the patio until I can't. It's going to be such a special time for him. When do you think you'd like to join us, Dear?"

"Would it be too soon to come at around four-fifteen or four-thirty?" she asked.

"Absolutely not; come as soon after four as you can. You'll see his car in my driveway - that's all you need to know to come on in."

Jerica's heart pounded in anticipation of this meeting. That night, she could barely sleep thinking about the party, about seeing Cole again. When daylight came, she looked at the pale pink dress she'd decided to wear then set pink sandals next to it in preparation. The hours were going to find a way to drag by and she decided to take a drive in her car, somewhere away from Mystic so that she wouldn't run into Cole and spoil his birthday surprise. She drove through neighboring towns and stopped at a small antique shop in Stonington where she found a pretty piece of blue glass to take home to her mother. When it grew closer to three o'clock, Jerica headed back to the hotel where she would dress and prepare for this longed for visit.

At four-twenty, Jerica drove slowly toward Mary's house where she saw both Cole's and Jim's cars parked in the driveway. She hesitated and pulled her car in next to Jim's. Quietly, apprehensively, she stepped out of the car, gathered her gift together, and walked toward the rear of Mary's home and patio. Mary saw her first and gasped as she covered her mouth with her hands. At that point, Cole and Jim turned and saw her, their eyes wide and their mouths half open. Mary cried as she walked toward Jerica with her arms extended.

"Let me hold him," she said as Jerica willingly placed Mary's dark haired grandchild into her arms.

Jerica stood statue still, but she laughed as little Jack tugged at his grandmother's thick, gray hair. Cole stood still also, and then he walked to the eight month old baby and kissed his hair. He turned and looked at Jerica. He wanted to ask why she hadn't told him, but then it didn't seem so important. What was important was that she was here. He walked to Jerica and, while guests arrived, he embraced her and practically devoured her with his kisses.

"He's the image of Cole as a baby," Mary said over and over to each guest, "and he's so like my John as well. A grandbaby, I have a grandbaby," she repeated with tears of joy.

Cole pulled Jerica aside. "I'm so sorry you had to go through this alone. I would have been there, Jerica. I had no idea. He's amazing and he's beautiful, just like his mother."

"And he's bright, handsome, and funny, just like his father. I couldn't think of a better gift to bring you than your son, John Michael McGinnis, Jack."

"My dad's name, and Michael is my middle name too, you know."

"Yes, I do know," Jerica said with a smile.

When everyone had dined and celebrated until past ten that evening, the house grew quiet as Mary rocked her grandson and loved watching him sleep in her arms.

Cole walked with Jerica out to the patio and said, "Will you come with me for a few minutes? I'd like to show you something."

Jerica leaned into him and said, "Cole, I will go anywhere with you."

They drove the short distance to Cole's house which Jerica almost didn't recognize. "When did you add a front porch?" she asked.

"Mom told me you loved the porches in North Carolina and that someday you hoped to have a home with a front porch, rockers and all. I wanted you to want to live here, for this to be your house, our home."

Jerica felt the tears well up in her eyes. "I accept," she said as their embrace entwined them, heart and soul.

Recipe for French Pancakes

In a bowl, blend
2 cups of flour
1 ½ cups of sugar
½ tsp. of salt
*Combine dry ingredients thoroughly

Add
¼ cup of melted butter
1 cup of milk

Stir until blended.

Add
5 eggs – beaten

Mix all ingredients together.
Fry in butter.
Add salt and butter to taste.

www.ingramcontent.com/pod-product-compliance
Lightning Source LLC
Chambersburg PA
CBHW050941120626
46552CB00001B/322